ROWENA DAWN

LEAP OF FAITH

Scarlet Leaf

2016

I hope you enjoy this book,

Rowena Dawn

This is a work of fiction.
Names, characters, places and incidents are products of the author's imagination and are not to be construed as real. Any resemblance to actual events, locales, organizations or persons, living or dead, is entirely coincidental.

SCARLET LEAF
TORONTO ONTARIO CANADA
COPYRIGHT BY ROWENA DAWN
ISBN: 9781988397283

I dedicate this book to Olesea and Lucia because they always make me feel young

Table of Contents

CHAPTER I

That's it. Now, I have to admit it. I'm stuck in a rut. Besides, I'm pretty sure that I'm a bit down. There's no way around that.

It's no wonder that sometimes I feel like I'm surrounded by a void and that I have lost my ability to connect with people. I think that's a pity. I was good at that, quite good, and that helped me in my career along the way.

The other day, for instance, I got out of bed early in the morning. That's my routine and I seem to be very fond of routine. For a while, I just stood near the window and listened to the deep quietness of the house. I didn't hear anything, not even a crack in the furniture. There wasn't even a moth in the air. But for my neighbor's small dog, which was yapping with enthusiasm in the yard across the street, I could have believed that I was the only breathing person on earth. I must say it wasn't such a delightful thought. Quite creepy, if you want to take my word on it.

I poured my first cup of coffee and sipped it slowly. I savored the hot black liquid while watching the street absently.

I let my mind wander everywhere and to everything without a specific purpose. I didn't stop to consider any thought. I was feeling depressed. Thinking about browsing my agenda full of meetings brought me further down so I decided to ignore it.

Suddenly, a thought popped in my mind. I wondered when I lost that feeling of eagerness that was there all the time. It accompanied my every step while I was climbing that metaphorical ladder that would have landed me into one of those legendary offices, stretching there, on the top floor of the company, sharing the view of the lake.

This morning, everything was different though. I woke up with a new feeling of expectation. It was almost close to anxiety. Now, that was something I hadn't felt in a very long time.

I knew that something was supposed to happen. I couldn't say if it was something good or bad but that didn't seem very important. At least I knew that something new lay ahead. I was giddy with anxiety and impatience as I was already sick of identical days. I was more than ready to try something new.

This time around, I drank my coffee watching the street with different eyes and I even enjoyed the antics of the small Russell terrier across the street. That was definitely new. Usually, he annoyed me with all that fuss he was making. He would run around like a headless chicken, chasing his tail, or some imaginary ghosts across the lawn. He'd constantly hunt the little birds brave enough to rest on the fence. His yapping competed with a fire alarm at times, and made you think that the end of the world was close. One thing was certain. He was the source of the sudden and persistent migraines which plagued me constantly.

Yet, today, I looked at him and I thought he was just full of life. It was as if he conveyed his joy of life to me somehow, and I felt energized. My brain was on alert and my blood was humming.

When I drove my car out of the garage, the feeling that new possibilities lay in front of me was still there with me and that was the first time in a long while that I'd felt something different than boredom.

CHAPTER 2

The morning dragged on as usual. As always, it even seemed endless, but that premonition that something new awaited ahead helped me to keep my good mood.

I almost got into trouble during my last meeting before lunch. I was bored to tears with the discussion subjects. We were always talking about the same problems over and over again. We never reached any conclusion anyway.

It seemed like a waste of time. I felt that we were having those meetings just to say that we were doing some work.

I found myself day-dreaming and someone asked me a question. Apparently, it was an important one, and I didn't even notice. To answer was out of question. Only when I felt everyone's eyes on me, and saw my boss's unpleasant scowl – the one he put on every time someone screwed up, I got back to the real world and gathered my scattered thoughts from wherever they had gone.

It wasn't any wonder that he asked me into his office for a short discussion afterwards. A few years ago, I would have been afraid if he'd called me to a meeting like that, especially because of his tone. That was the tone one would hear whenever he was ready to tell someone that their services were no longer required in the company.

For a brief moment then, I thought of the pink slip that was offered when someone was fired, but I shrugged it off as if I hadn't given a damn about anything. It wasn't just a front. Right then, I didn't really care. I thought that probably, my depression was deeper than I thought and I got to that point where

I started having self-destructive tendencies.

He showed me into his office and he motioned me to sit in the armchair beside his mocha sofa. With a nod of my head, I took a seat and waited patiently for him to start talking. I looked around and cringed. The soft tones of the sofa and armchair clashed with bold and crude paintings on the wall. My boss's taste was far from cultivated.

"Meg, you've been with us for several years now," he told me evenly.

It was an interesting beginning. But what could I have said? I nodded my assent and waited for him to continue.

Something was there to be said, I knew it, and when Mr. Johnson was talking, people had to listen. So I stoically had to listen to what he had to say.

"I think you've reached your maximum of potential here, Meg."

Yep, the pink slip seemed to become more real by the second. It was like I'd had it in my hand. I could feel the texture of that thin pink paper that had the bad habit of appearing in people's nightmares and stress them out.

I had a friend who had had sleepless nights after such dreams haunted him. He was afraid to even close his eyes. He was terrified that the same dream would come back again and again to torment him. In the end, if I am not wrong, he was sacked after a while. He wasn't efficient anymore because of sleep deprivation and had become a liability. So, his dreams came true and he got that malefic pink slip.

"I don't want to say that you haven't done a good job here. Far from me that," he said.

All right, I made a note to myself: he wanted to give me a little good-bye speech. I resigned myself to listen to it. It wasn't like I'd had something better to do and I couldn't just stand up and walk away. I was too polite to behave like that and it was a matter of respect, after all.

It was true that I still had those pesky afternoon meetings. It was as if I had gone from one meeting to another those days. There was also that promise I had made to Lorna to have lunch with her, but I could be late for once. It was not such a big deal as I had never been late for a thing in my life before. People would live with that too.

"I was thinking that you needed something a little more challenging... Something that would motivate you again," Mr. Johnson continued.

That was quite a good speech to be delivered when someone was fired. Tell people that you let them go only to give them the possibility to fulfill themselves, to reach their full potential in another job, somewhere else. Good thinking, boss! Did you get trained for that or what?

"I know it might seem somewhat surprising for you now..."

Actually, no, it wasn't surprising at all. Probably people had become aware that I was bored to tears with the same job that didn't offer me any challenge anymore, and had become only a chore for me.

One thing was important though. I knew that losing my job wouldn't be a serious problem for me right then. A few years before, it would have been a calamity.

I hadn't been on a vacation for a few years now and I deserved some spare time for myself. I had enough money in the bank to live well even if I didn't have a job for a while. I didn't have to pay rent because a very old and almost unknown aunt had left me the house I was living in, and my wardrobe was full of clothes I hadn't had a chance to wear before. If I analyzed things calmly, I didn't eat too much so ... – no, it would not be a real problem, at least for a while.

After some time, I will see. It wasn't like I'd had to make a crucial decision right then. I'd have had enough time on my hands afterwards.

"I see that you seem distressed and thoughtful…"

How could he see that? I wasn't distressed at all. I felt only like I'd been somehow suspended in the air. Suddenly, I had no plans for tomorrow. Wow, it had been a long time since I'd had such a day stretched before my eyes. A normal day meant that everything had to be carefully planned out and I had to respect that schedule to the minute or hell would have frozen over.

"But believe me, Meg, it is a fantastic opportunity," he continued, although I had stopped listening to him and his words were just some noise in the background. I'd catch one here and there and I thought it was enough.

Don't tell me it's a real opportunity, boss, because I know it. Not a lot to do, I admit, but there was a lot of potential for change. I could have tried some club for knitting – yeah, I was joking. I had never been able to do that. However, I had always wanted to pass over that handicap. I remember my grandma had tried to teach me until she found out that I was a lost cause. Maybe now it was the right time to start again. I might feel some fulfillment if I managed to do something out of the ordinary. Of course, out of the ordinary for me.

"To run a new branch, though as little as that one might be quite challenging, you know," he said.

Whoa, rewind, boss, please. I think I have lost some of the things that he said on the way and now his speech didn't make sense at all. Bad, very bad not to pay attention, Meg! How did he get from firing me to having me run a new office?

I'm afraid I should go and see a doctor. Do I have memory loss or blackouts? Something did happen; this is certain. Even though I didn't listen attentively, something must have registered in my mind.

I coughed to find my voice and said, "Could you give me more details, please? You were talking about a branch…"

"Well, I thought you knew about the new branch we're opening in France," he said a little startled. "We've talked about it quite often... Remember the last few meetings we've had... You know the language very well, Meg, better than anyone in the office, and of course you've worked with us for over ten years, and your performance has been amazing so far... it was only normal to choose you for the direction of this branch, Meg. I thought you'd be aware that we'd choose you to run that office," he continued and seemed dumbfounded that I was completely unaware of that.

All right, it was true that I had known about that new position for manager at the Paris branch, and for some time now. Yet, I had thought that they were going to choose someone from over there, so I hadn't even bothered thinking about that.

"I appreciate the offer, of course! I am even flattered that you chose me, but wouldn't it have been better to hire someone more familiar with the city and the business scene?"

Damn, my stupid honesty! I think I've just traded my dream-trip to France because of that! I felt like slapping myself over the face and I will certainly do it lately when I'm alone in my office. Why can't I keep my mouth shut at least once?

"We might, of course, but I know, I am even convinced that you'll manage very well in Paris, considering what you've realized within the company so far. Of course, we hired a guy from there to help you out there with advice and inside knowledge... I know we aren't offering you much time, but we need you there within two weeks, Meg. We didn't expect that everything would go so well and that we'd be able to open the branch so fast, because otherwise we'd have told you sooner. So, what do you think? Could you do it? Could you be there so soon?"

Could I? It wasn't such a difficult question. The answer wasn't so easy, though. There were many things that I had to take into consideration before committing to leave in two weeks.

So, let's rewind this again: in the morning I didn't know what to do to change my life, and I was stuck in a rut that suffocated me, effectively. Now, my life was taking a new path. This new direction was so altered that I couldn't even recognize it anymore. This was the moment I'd been waiting for and I would have been really stupid not to grasp it with both hands.

"I'll manage, don't worry," I said quickly, afraid that he might change his mind if he noticed my uncertainty.

Was I saying those words? Was I crazy or what? The monotony had definitely burnt my brain cells. Was I able to arrange everything and leave to the other side of the ocean in only two weeks? God, I did love short deadlines, didn't I? It was like I was living only for them.

I smiled nicely at my dear old boss and turned towards the door to leave fast, so that he couldn't change his mind and give that opportunity to someone else.

"Of course, you'll have to show Marcy all of the stuff you've been working on so that she could take over for you," his words stopped me exactly when I was about to step out of the door.

I turned back to him and nodded. After that, I finally managed to leave his office without any other interruptions.

Walking slowly to my office, I started daydreaming. All I could see before my eyes were snapshots from various movies: Paris by night, Gene Kelly dancing with the Eiffel Tower in the background, Audrey Hepburn...

Suddenly, realizing what I was doing, I shook my head and woke up. God, I was acting like a schoolgirl who was offered a romantic night in town for the first time! I shook myself mentally and thought: all right, girl, think! There'd be work, even a lot of work, actually, if you started thinking as you should! There'd be sleepless nights and headaches over one thing or another.

I knew it as well as I knew that I was sick of what I was doing at that moment in time. I knew that I could not go on with the same routine anymore. I needed a change and this was the right way out. Or, maybe, I was still day-dreaming. What if? That would be great. Was I losing it or what?

I decided to go along with my day and see what else would come up. So, I went to get ready to meet Lorna for lunch. I was already five minutes late and I needed at least ten to get to the restaurant where we were supposed to meet.

CHAPTER 3

I ducked into my office to take my bag when Susan, my personal assistant, came after me with glee in her eyes.

"Congrats, Meg! Everyone has heard that you were going to take over the management of the office we're opening in Paris!"

I smiled at her with a lot of warmth. My smile wasn't only for her congratulations, although they were also welcome, but because she was the living proof that I hadn't lost it yet. I was not day-dreaming and I had no blackouts.

So everything turned out to be real, as real as it could get. That was truly great!

Now, I had to start making plans for my move. I didn't even know where I was going to live there, or what I was going to do with the house here. That was a real challenge but I knew I could deal with everything as I always had.

"You know, Mr. Johnson sent me the memo explaining everything they've arranged about your accommodations in Paris and… well, everything else. They rented you a splendid little cottage in the suburbs. You know, the *'banlieue'*."

Yes, I should have known that he would have taken care to rent a house for me, because, as a rule, he was very attentive with such details. Yet, I felt tricked somehow. I'd have liked to look for a house myself. I didn't think they'd already done it for me. Big mistake! I had to start thinking ahead.

I knew very well Mr. Johnson's taste. I had seen my boss's house as well, not only his office. The house was full of horrible modern things and kitsch.

I'd have preferred something a bit out of fashion, European, refined, something that would remind me of the beginning of the twentieth century or even about the end of the nineteenth. I wanted to see that Paris I had read so much about when I was a student.

Shrugging, I gave up pining about the choices I'd have made. It wouldn't have done any good to me longing for something I couldn't change. I should have known they wouldn't have sent me there within two weeks without taking care of everything there. The company was very thoughtful with such matters.

As there was nothing more for me to do there then, I headed out. I had to get to the restaurant where I was supposed to meet Lorna for lunch.

CHAPTER 4

"I can't believe you! Paris! You've always been the lucky one! Not like me! I've been behind the eight ball all my life," Lorna cried out, suffocated by jealousy.

All right, a wretched beginning, then! Yet, I should have expected it. I should have known that Lorna would look at everything only in relation to her. She had never been able to be happy for someone else. I should have seen it coming. I should have imagined that she would whine and be upset she wasn't in my shoes.

Lorna was my cousin though, and that was why I was trying to get along with her. *"Family always comes first,"* grandpa used to say. *"They are annoying sometimes, and most of them are petty and unbearable, but they are your family and you have my sense of duty, so you'd be able to put up with them quite well, I think."*

Thanks, grandpa, for passing on your sense of duty. I would have preferred to inherit something else: maybe a house on the shore of the ocean. Heritage is so bothersome sometimes.

I listened to Lorna's complaints and whining during the entire lunch. She whined about her last relationship that had just ended. I suppose the guy had had enough of her constant whining and cut his losses short. Then, she complained about her job. It didn't present any perspectives to her anymore and she was sick of it. She also whined that she couldn't afford to renew her winter wardrobe. As if everybody had to change all their clothes every season. In a few words, she grumbled about everything that was going on in her life and she expected nothing less but my commiserating with her.

I knew beforehand that this lunch would be like that, but once a month I have to be brave and listen to her. She was family after all and one doesn't shun family!

I wonder why was I complaining about my loneliness. Sometimes it's a blessing in disguise, I swear to God. Anything is better than to have to listen to such an incessant lamentation.

The moment I stood up and said bye to Lorna, my thoughts went back to Paris and my possible life there, which, of course, would have to be wonderful. It wasn't possible otherwise. It was Paris after all.

Paris is the city for love and I hadn't had that for a long time, actually since I left that huge ego that competed with the size of Texas, named Mitchell. He was the type of man that lived with the impression that he was God's gift on earth for women and he played the part without flaw. Everything was about him. Everything was for him, and the woman at his arm or in his bed was only an annex whose existence was reduced to what she could do for him. She was needed only to enhance his status and satisfy some of his needs. Feelings never came into the equation. They were meant to burden only middle class people, whom he considered as part of the bourgeoisie. I took exception to his credo and decided to split.

But let's put his memory aside as it wasn't a very happy one in fact. It's better to get back to Paris. The great and romantic town! Everybody knows that Paris is for dreaming and comfort! For strolls and afternoon delights in small bistros or for smelling the flowers!

CHAPTER 5

Finally, here was Paris! I'd just landed and a car had been waiting for me at the airport to drive me to my new house.

I looked around and I couldn't believe my eyes. It was a shock to my entire system. I wondered where was the town I'd been reading about in all those novels I couldn't put aside.

There was a lot of litter in the street, and I could hear an infernal noise through the window of the car. The decibels were off the scale. The traffic was exactly as at home, if not worse! I was afraid during the entire ride home because I wasn't sure that I'd get in one piece to my destination.

I tried to find my heart and I pushed myself mentally, *'don't dare to get disappointed! It is just a first impression after a long flight and sometimes first impressions lie. Wait and see!'*

I was right! Indeed, first impressions may be misleading sometimes. The little cottage that had been rented for me was everything I'd have ever wanted. My boss's taste was nowhere in sight, so probably he'd given the initial orders, but the people he hired knew how to choose. The atmosphere from the beginning of the twentieth century was exactly what I'd imagined.

The cottage was cozy and somehow rustic. It had a certain atmosphere about it. It was refreshing. It felt like home in a way. It welcomed me with warmth. Here and there, one could see it'd been renovated over the years and I was pretty sure that there was history encrusted in those walls. I wondered what my history would be like. The next day my life there would start officially and I'd see from there.

Now I felt tired to the bones. It had been two weeks of a whirlwind that seemed endless at times. I was exhausted because I'd been trying to solve everything in time so that I would be able to leave without delay. After an eight-hour flight between the two continents, everything settled in. I felt wrung off.

Nonetheless, at the same time, I felt fulfilled and satisfied. I was eager to start my new work. It had been a long time since I waited to have that feeling again.

I felt enthusiastic because I knew that following day would be the first day of the rest of my life and I couldn't wait to see what would come. I was happy that I was exhausted because otherwise I couldn't have slept. Impatience would have made me restless. Even though I was told that no one expected to see me at the office the next day, I couldn't wait for daylight to come, so that I could go and see my new office. Obviously, I wouldn't want to look like a scarecrow, and for that, I needed eight hours of sleep.

CHAPTER 6

The deception hit me hard the following morning when I saw that the rest of my life didn't turn out to be as great as I'd expected, unfortunately! That was what happened when expectations didn't live up to reality, and disappointments came one after another.

The first person I had the pleasure to meet in my new office was Ian. He was the expert that my company had hired to be my advisor. I had to admit that the encounter with him was a total shock for my system.

Ian was a huge hunk of a dark-haired Irishman. His height would have competed only with his ego. He had plenty of that. Ian considered that he obviously knew everything better than I did and that meant that my little head might have exploded into millions of pieces if I'd tried to think for myself!

Much worse than that, my heart skipped a beat whenever I laid my eyes on him. He had dark grey eyes, which shadowed his thoughts. I never knew if he was laughing at me or if he wanted only to be polite. Ian had thick eyebrows, as dark as his full head of hair which seemed untamable, even though he brushed it. He was well build and his broad shoulders looked like they had come from my most hidden fantasies.

Everything attracted me to him like a magnet. That was true. However, his generous mouth, with lips begging to be tasted thoroughly, could arouse me so hard that it pushed me over the edge. That wasn't such a good thing considering my position in the management.

I had to give myself a good shake to get back to reality and start behaving professionally. I was sure I would have been committed into that hospital with happy people if I had jumped him as a woman desperate because she hadn't seen a good looking guy for a long while.

He was a delight for my eyes, that Ian. Yet, I would have preferred to have as an advisor someone that wouldn't have woken any feelings or sensations inside me. It wasn't like I could have acted based on such feelings. It was better if there was no temptation to interfere with my duties.

My personal assistant, Mireille, who, in principle, was supposed to work for me, was looking at him as if he'd been a God who descended on earth and every single word coming out of his mouth came directly from the Bible. She looked at him but, from what I saw, most of the time, her eyes followed Philippe, the manager of the investments department, although I wasn't very sure that he man knew the real meaning of the word "investments". Yet, that was another story and I

predicted that one day I'd have to take care of that as well.

It looked like I'd have to make Mireille understand that I was the one that was calling the shots in that office. She didn't seem to be aware of that. If she didn't like it, then I would have to fire her, because I didn't see any other choice.

After the first week, I was so sick of everyone in the office that I could scream. There were moments when I could howl at the moon like a lonely wolf. Yet, I was afraid that if I'd started howling I wouldn't have stopped and then I would have been in serious trouble.

The manager of the investments department, Philippe, Mireille's passion, was a French guy. He also had the impression that he was God's gift to women on earth, another Mitchell in sight. He might have been dressed in the fashion of another continent, but he was the same.

I felt dizzy when I realized that I had to deal with the same type of man again! He almost drawled every single word he was saying, like he had tossed it through honey first. Soon I got to the point that I would get a toothache whenever I heard him talking.

Philippe looked at every woman who was crossing his path with puppy eyes and it was disturbing but his tactics seemed to be effective. I couldn't believe my eyes when I noticed that he'd sweep women of their feet, regardless of age or social background just be glancing at them. Probably, that was why Philippe was somewhat successful in his field. It was clear that his success wasn't the result of his intelligence or his knack for investments. Those were in short supply.

Nevertheless, when he realized that his tactics didn't work with me, Philippe became bitter and spiteful. He resented me deeply and his behavior towards me changed completely. As if I'd cared!

CHAPTER 7

I sometimes wondered how I could have been so sad about being alone and about having to do the same damn thing every damn day. It seemed like heaven whenever I looked back now. It was a pity that I hadn't known how to appreciate what I had.

Now, the only moments I had for myself were two hours at night, but in order to have those two hours, of course, I had to sleep less to create a reserve.

All the other time I had left, I had to fight over everything and with everyone. I fought with my Irish advisor because nothing I'd say counted. He knew the business scene in Paris better than I. I fought my personal assistant. Everything Ian or

Philippe would say was important and I was just some extra baggage in the office. That made her ignore me and my requests all the time. Nonetheless, I fought with my managers. They were all French and that was why they knew better how to deal with things in Paris.

At one point, I arrived to the conclusion that God hated me. At first, I'd had those idiot feelings for weeks at a time, when the only thing I was craving was a radical change, and now I was living in that continuous nightmare that made me wish that things would go back to normal.

Whoever said that one should be careful what they wished for was right. I also wished for something but I got more than I bargained for. Days were a continuous fight to make myself heard and listened to, even just a little. I was aware that my decisions weren't respected even half of the time, no matter how much I'd have insisted on it.

Beside that continuous and tiresome fight, I also had to control my impulses towards Ian, and this was just driving me crazy. I was behaving like a teenager. Whenever I'd see him, my heart would start beating faster. My hands would get all sweaty and my thoughts would get so confused that I didn't even know whether I was going or coming or what I wanted to say or do. That meant that I didn't have a prayer to hope that I could make him to heed my decisions.

What I needed was to find a way to stop my childish attraction to him. It wasn't like I could have done something about it. I couldn't have asked him if he wanted to meet somewhere out in town or have lunch or dinner together. When everything was said and done, I was still in the manager's position and he was just one of my employees and something like that just wasn't done. It would go under the sexual harassment header and might lead to an ugly court trial for the company.

That was why I had to keep all my feelings under lock and key and train my face so that no one could read anything. My feelings were meant to be kept under lock and key.

CHAPTER 8

Now it was clear. There was no such thing as love in Paris! Maybe it was just something like the love I felt for Ian, a hopeless love. Everything else was just business.

I wonder how I could have ever believed that love awaited at every turn, on every corner. There were only interests, smaller or bigger fights in the shadows and if you weren't tough enough, you were swept out of the business scene immediately.

Paris wasn't for romantic and weak creatures, not that I'd be the romantic or weak kind, truth to be told. I wasn't a romantic and I had sharpened my claws long time ago. After all, I'd trained on other scenes and I'd already succeeded in a man's world. There was no way I'd let myself defeated by a bunch of men with an ego bigger than Everest or some women that still lived one century behind and didn't hear of the feminist movement.

***

Christmas was around the corner and I longed for familiar faces and the scent of the fir tree and the aroma of my Grandma's pudding. I felt the void growing around me more and more every day and now, I understood better why some people hated holidays. I was one of their club now.

Anyway, this year, only a fir tree would connect me to my past and happy life. I didn't have enough time available to go back home and spend Christmas with the few family members I still had. I wouldn't have returned to Paris in time for the whole bunch of problems that must be solved before the end of the year...

***

Two weeks before Christmas, my weekend was a busy one. I wandered everywhere around the city, until I hunted down the perfect tree. Then, I started decorating my little cottage exactly in the way I wanted and that lifted my mood a bit more. I had been feeling depressed lately and I had felt the urge to do something to cheer up a little.

I put aside any of the thoughts related to work and the problems created by the people in the office. I thought that having one weekend just for myself couldn't do any harm. Monday was close enough and I knew it would take its toll on me.

CHAPTER 9

On the following Friday, I decided to take all my power back. It was mine after all and I had to put my foot down and make it happen. It was high time I'd done it already. I'd been procrastinating for too long and that didn't do any good. It was the right moment to assume leadership and if I hadn't been able to do it, then clearly my place wasn't there. I would have to return to New York with my tail between my legs and throw in the towel. Well, that wasn't a too pleasant option for me, to be honest.

I was already sick of being taken as a fool and being dismissed because I was either a woman or a foreigner, so I let everyone know that I would have separate meetings with the middle and high management staff during the day. That didn't seem to stay quite right with most of them.

First, I called my Irish advisor in my office for a discussion. Truth to be told, he had kept bothering me since day one for various reasons but I didn't want to dwell too much on those reasons.

That was a continuous fight for me and I was aware that I was about to lose sooner or later. I had to try hard not to think of him too much. I tried hard not to remember that mop of hair that seemed to implore my fingers to touch it or that mouth that corrupted and led to sin. I had to grow up and deal with the matters at hand.

"I think you know why I invited you here for a discussion today," I began my discussion with Ian on a resolute tone because I was determined not to show him that he had a terrible effect on my system.

"To discuss the possible investments for the next year or to discuss in what stage are the ones we've made so far," Ian ventured to guess, but I shook my head.

"Neither one. I want to have a talk with you about the extent of your attributions within the company… I want you to understand that, actually, I am in charge of this branch, I run the show, and your position within the company requires only consulting. You are here to advise, and that's all. Consequently, you are not to make decisions on my behalf and you are not to manage the staff as long as I'm able to do it. Taking decision and handling staff are my tasks, Ian, and only mine. As long I'm not incapacitated otherwise, I intend to carry them out myself. That was the purpose for my appointment at the head of the office here. If you can't deal with this situation, and you can't carry on with your job within these parameters, or you think that the system is too rigid for you, then I am ready to accept your resignation right now. It isn't a problem," I told him with resolve even though I felt a twist in my heart at the thought that he'd be leaving the firm.

That meant that I couldn't see him anymore. Moreover, that added to my regret of losing him in his capacity of advisor. It would have been a great loss because his abilities in the field were high.

Ian had proved over and over again that he was a wise man and he knew how to do his job. He was able to see the big picture and never made decisions based only on what he had before his eyes.

He was a good chess player, which made him able to determine in advance what moves his adversary would make and react in consequence. Nevertheless, what hurt more was that I couldn't have seen him daily. I knew I was behaving like a teenager eager to see her idol furtively but I couldn't change that. Probably, I was compensating for the times when I should have behaved like that but I had been too busy building a career.

When he heard my words, that ironic smile that made him looked amused most of the time and was so characteristic to him, appeared on his lips again. It was something gradual. First the left corner of his mouth would twitch a bit and then the smile would flourish and throw a strong blow to my heart.

It was a powerful weapon that smile of his. It had the power to make me melt, but not this time. now it irritated me and I wondered what he found so funny in what I was saying. Maybe he was thinking I was joking or that I wasn't capable to stand by my decisions, and that was something I couldn't brush off easily. So I asked him quarrelsome, "Do you think I'm kidding?"

I was aware that I asked my question argumentatively. I was tensed and ready for a full tirade, but Ian put up his hand to stop me and replied calmly, "Oh, I am sure you're serious, Meg, don't worry. I've learnt that you're not the kind of person that opens her mouth just to say something, to fill in the silence. In fact, this is something I really admire in you. Now, back to the discussion at hand. It's not an issue for me if you're the one calling the shots around here, Meg. As a matter of fact, in my opinion, that's something you should have done some time ago. I stepped in and made decisions on your behalf up to now only because I thought that you needed help to find your way in a new environment. Now, I can see that's not the case anymore, and I can step aside so that you could do your job... I only hope you won't regret that you've rushed into this decision... I hope it is not too soon for you and that you're ready for what will come, Meg," he continued pensively.

Oh, God, I wished he had sat down, so that he wouldn't look at me from above. Nevertheless, from the beginning of our conversation he'd chosen to stand and unfortunately, he was a very tall man. I reached only somewhere at his chest.

It didn't feel good to have someone looking down to you like that. Now it was much worse because he was the only man able to short-circuit my system with ease whenever we interacted.

In such situations, when he was too close to me, and especially when we were alone in a room, I always became aware that he was far too tall for me. He was at least one foot taller, I think. He was also big everywhere: broad shoulders and big hands – yep, surely women would die to have such a guy for themselves, and I'd stand in line waiting for my turn even though not too peacefully.

Now it was clear that all my grey cells had gone crazy and my hormones had taken the driver seat, which was not what I had planned for that meeting. He seemed in total control of the room and that was exactly the opposite of what I had wanted to happen. I disliked the situation deeply and probably, that was why I reacted more fancifully than I should have.

"So, should I understand that you're going to stay with the firm?"

"For the moment, why not?" Ian replied shrugging with indifference. "I am only an adviser here, as you have pointed out so nicely. I definitely don't have any problems taking my orders from you. It is a blessing to let you deal with the staff. It will mean less work and trouble for me, evidently, and I welcome that. Now, I can't say that I know what I'll decide in the future, of course, but I'll make sure to let you know."

Oh! So he wanted to say that so far, he'd been working hard doing my job as well not only his. I felt my eyes narrowing to slits. That always happened when I was irritated. It didn't escape my notice that he was aware of that trait of mine, because his smile widened more. Despite my rising ire, that made me pay much more attention to those lips that had appeared in every one of my fantasies for the last few weeks. Then, his smile took a naughtier turn and that made my blood boil. I was beyond furious now.

Ian was a good-looking bastard but that didn't mean that I had to lie down and accept his sardonic behavior. But what could I have said? It wasn't as if I could have snapped and reprimanded him.

In all honesty, he hadn't said anything to cross the line between the two of us. He only smiled and, unfortunately, regardless of my position in the company, I couldn't fire someone for smiling, no matter what that smile meant and how it made me feel.

I felt handled once more, and this time with only a smile. That didn't sit too well with me and it wasn't a nice feeling altogether. So, enough was enough. I tried to shake the awkwardness of the situation and told him that the meeting was over. He acknowledged my dismissal with a nod.

As soon as he had left the room, still smiling, damn it, I tried to pull myself together and I called Philippe to come into my office.

Philippe was our little gigolo, slash marketing director who lived under the mistaken impression that no woman on earth could be immune to his charm, no matter her age, social condition or intellectual level.

Well, I was the exception. I didn't melt when he smiled at me. His smile didn't do the same things to me as Ian's did, thank God! One was enough for a cerebral woman like me who prided herself with being a reasonable person.

Whenever Philippe smiled at me, I felt like something was crawling all over my skin. It was a slimy feeling. His eyes had nothing to tell me. They only annoyed me whenever I'd catch him staring at me. I loathed those languorous glances he would practice on women.

I had a completely different sensation when Ian stared at me. Is smile would make me tingle all over and my temperature would go high.

Philippe came into my office and smiled at me condescendingly, which wasn't something totally new. He'd usually do that whenever I called him to my office. The reason of the meeting wouldn't have mattered. I'd noticed, and more than once, that that smile made him look annoyed as if the poor man had suffered immensely. His pain could be related to the unwanted intrusion in his life. He left the impression that, without such mundane intrusions, his life would have been a full of passion and challenges.

This time, again, he was trying to convey the message that it was his choice to be there. He was always keen on leaving the impression that no one could dictate anything to him and especially not me.

For him, my presence in the firm represented only a mere nuisance. He considered that I had gotten that job as a sinecure and, consequently, he bothered to pay attention to me in the same way one would pay attention to a three-year old child's tantrum.

That behavior annoyed me. Sick of his demeanor and to clarify the parameters of the discussion from the beginning, I started in force, "Philippe, I have to let you know that I'm dissatisfied with your activity within the company in general and with your approach to business, in particular. Not once did you do what you were asked to do. I have to note that all the directions you took all by yourself brought little success overall if any at all. Too many failures have been recorded lately because of your performance or lack thereof and the company has registered serious losses. We could have avoided at least 90 percent of them. I can't do otherwise but to give you a warning right now. If you want to keep your position here, in our company, then you have to learn how to work in a team and how to follow my lead. This is why I am here: to offer you a direction of action and to verify your competence, so that your failures get reduced and the branch starts bringing in profit."

I noticed the changes on his face. He was getting redder and redder with anger. I was sure he couldn't have imagined in his weirdest dreams that someone – especially a little woman, as I was – I am just five two, to be truthful, could speak to him like that and bring light over his incompetence.

"Don't you think you should leave things like directions to me?" he asked haughtily with a hint of contempt in his voice once he regained his speech.

So, I was right all the time. Philippe thought that I was a brainless woman that couldn't do anything important. Probably, he imagined I'd been promoted in that position by sleeping with the boss and that was why he used to measure me from head to toes in that shameless manner all the time, as if I had been an object that could be bought for a ridiculous amount.

"No, I don't think so, but the opposite," I replied in an even voice. "Of course, if you have any problems with my management, the door is behind you, Philippe. Don't let it kick you on your way out! It's not an issue for us to let you go because I am sure we could find someone as competent as you if not better and quite fast. In fact, I don't foresee any trouble in doing just that."

"Are you sure you could find the best leads as I do?!! I have experience and…"

"Yes, yes, yes… I know," I interrupted his tirade waving my hand impatiently. "I've seen your resume, Philippe. It seems as if it had come straight from a fairy tale. On the other hand, I do have the necessary experience," I stressed out the words. "In spite of your rich imagination, which I'm sure helps you keep this grand image you have about yourself, I did work hard to get into this position in the company and I do have the necessary flair for business, don't worry about it. I am pretty sure that this company can do without you quite well and can even get much further without your help which was inexistent up to now."

His eyes bulged and he tried to say something but I put my hand up suddenly stopping him which gave me the chance to see him getting madder than before. His eyes were sparking with anger and all the signs were there showing that his hand tingled ready to slap me. I could read it in his eyes. He wanted very bad to show me what he thought about me and my words, considering the way he was flexing his fists.

"I want you to go back into your office and think things over again and very well. You have this entire weekend to make a decision about what you want in the future. It is your last chance, Phillippe. On Monday, I expect you here, in my office, at ten sharp. By then, you should already know if you intend to continue to work here or not. Of course, working here means that you'll follow my lead. Moreover, and I can't stress this enough, you'll leave the female employees alone and that starting from this moment on. I don't want to have any sexual harassment problems in the company and I'm afraid that, due to your behavior, that's where we're headed. Have I made myself clear?" I asked him in a sharp and decisive voice.

He nodded nervously that he understood and went out of my office furiously, slamming the door behind him. I couldn't care less that he lost his temper. Actually, I had even counted on that. Hadn't he lost his temper, it would have meant I didn't do my job properly and I'd just wasted my time.

I know I put up with his bad behavior and moods for far too long. It was the moment to take the lead on this problem once and for all, and solve all these issues that had consumed my days and nights. The only thing that bothered me was the thought that I'd procrastinated too long to do it. I should have done it sooner. The thought that I acted cowardly troubled me. I always thought I was a strong and independent woman but such a woman wouldn't have waited so long to bring an end to such a situation.

I put the thought aside because I still had something to do. Now, I had to finish with everything at once and have a complete coup within the branch. After I spoke to the other managers, I also asked my so-called personal assistant in my office for a discussion as well.

She entered looking at me as if I had suddenly grown two horns on my head. Disdain was pouring out from each pore of her body. Nonetheless, I could also smell her fear. She was sweating profusely something I'd never noticed before. It must have been something new.

For the first time, she was feeling something else for me besides scorn. I stared her down with cold eyes and waived my hand, showing her that she should sit down. It appeared that Philippe had already let her know what had happened in my office and I had clearly become enemy number one.

"Mireille, I am not sure you are aware who your boss is. You don't seem to know who is the person you work for, I mean. I'm afraid that I have to point out to you that neither Ian nor Philippe is in charge in this branch of the company. I am the one appointed at its direction and, furthermore, you're hired to work exclusively for me. If you can't grasp this concept and if you have difficulties to come to terms with this reality, then I will have no choice but to replace you. Of course, you will have the two-week notice stipulated in your contract, but nothing more, because, honestly, you don't deserve even that. Your overall assessment is extremely poor. You don't work as you should and the only thing you really do full time here is to flirt with the male personnel, which, by the way, is nowhere mentioned in your job description. When I give you a task, you choose not to hear me and even my agenda would be a real mess if I didn't take the trouble to keep it myself. Well, if I'm not wrong, this is actually one of your main duties. Reports I need are never ready on time, if they ever are, because up to now, I haven't seen a report written entirely by you. Whenever I look for you, I find you in Philippe's office and I simply can't fathom why you'd be there. As far as I know, you should be in his office only if I send you with a document there and I am pretty sure I've never done it yet. If you need to see him for personal reasons, you can do it while you're on break on your own time," I said in a crisp voice and waited for aa few seconds so that my words could settle in her mind. Then I continued, "Consequently, you have time until Monday to think everything over and decide what you want to do. Then, you'll let me know what you've chosen: working here or taking your last pay stub. Of course, if you decide to continue working here, then you have to make some radical changed. You have to do something to earn your pay, because we can't pay you just to waste your time. Have I made myself clear?" I asked her looking at her with determination.

She opened her mouth to say something but she couldn't utter a word. The next second, she burst into tears and ran out of my office as if she'd been chased by wolves.

Well, it seemed like a nice ending for my meetings that afternoon, I thought. I managed to get ironic smiles, macho replies and tears. That would cover the entire spectre of human emotions. I was pretty sure I hit 100 percent.

CHAPTER 10

Good, everything I had planned for during the last few days was taken care of in one way or another, so now I had only to write my weekly report for the mother company and then I could finally go home.

I couldn't wait for the weekend to begin. I was in a dire need of relaxation after such a long and grueling period full of tension. I'm not a very tough person, and in order to play that role I had to use a lot of strength. Now I was almost exhausted. I had very few reserves of energy left in my body.

After a quarter of an hour, I finally finished the report and called Mireille to ask her to prepare some things for Monday morning but, of course, no one answered. It wasn't uncommon, considering the fact that Mireille used to spend more time in other offices than hers. However, I didn't expect it to happen so soon after our recent discussion.

I went out of my office and saw that she'd fled her office again. Probably she was with Ian or Philippe because she had to look for a strong man to soothe her after everything I had told her during our meeting.

Decisively, I went to Ian office, and found him on the phone with one of our customers. I turned around to leave so that I wouldn't disturb him, but he waved me into the room and signaled me to wait for a moment, so I went inside his office. As I had nothing else to do, I took a seat on one of the comfortable chairs he had for guests in front of his desk. He'd chosen very comfortable chairs. It felt heavenly to relax in one of them. Evidently, I took advantage of the situation to watch him as much as I wanted.

He soon finished with his phone conversation and asked me, "Is there anything else that you wanted to say? Is there something that you forgot to cover during the discussion we had earlier?"

I felt that I was getting angry with him but I didn't raise to the net to take the ball and I made efforts to remain calm and composed. I thought that it seemed petty of him to touch on our previous subject of discussion in such a manner. It wasn't something I'd expected.

"I was just looking for Mireille, that is all, Ian," I said haughtily. "However, it seems that she's not here so I'd better go."

Ian smiled mockingly at me and then he replied, "Of course, she's not here. My office isn't her usual refuge when things get tough. I can bet you can find her in Philippe's office...," he said and then seemed lost in his thoughts for a few moments.

I even started to feel uncomfortable, like a voyeur and thought of leaving.

"Meg, I am still your advisor, aren't I?" Ian said hesitantly, gazing directly in my eyes. Hesitation wasn't something characteristic to him and my curiosity was picked.

"Yes, you are," I answered a little puzzled not knowing where he wanted to go with that line of conversation but I wanted him to continue so I continued to sit.

"Good!" he nodded and then tapped his hand on the desk. "Then, I advise you to fire her and as soon as possible. Mireille does nothing else all day but flirt with Philippe and that's it. That's the extent of her contribution. I'm pretty sure that this isn't why the company pays her. I'm not even sure whether she knows how to use a computer, to be truthful. Philippe hired her and she's loyal only to him, so that you know."

"I had the same idea!" I replied looking at him reproachfully, feeling like being reprimanded for not noticing what stood before my eyes.

He laughed and replied, "Yeah, I knew you'd think of that! From what

I've seen so far, you're a smart girl! You know what you have to do and don't really need pointers."

"Thank you, but this thing doesn't work with me, Ian" I replied curtly and stood up.

"What thing?" he frowned at my words.

"Flirting, flattering…"

"I am not Philippe!" Ian snapped at me furiously, cutting me off. At the same time, he also slapped the top of his desk. There wasn't any trace of smile in his sparkling eyes. He was furious and it was the first time I'd seen him like that. "If you don't mind, keep that in your mind. I'm not Philippe," he repeated again with more determination than before. "Don't think that I'd lower myself to playing such games, and especially with you, Meg! It's not me. It was just a praise for your abilities. If you don't need it or want it, no problem, I'll keep quiet from now on. I won't express my opinion in such matters, so that you don't feel like I was trying to flatter you," he said sarcastically. "Now, is there anything else to discuss, because if not, I have to go and see the guy from the perfume company, and I already should be on my way," he dismissed me coldly.

"No, there's nothing else," I answered back diffidently.

"Good, then! In my way out, I'll send Mireille to you, don't worry..." he said, standing up at his turn and taking a file in his hand, effectively showing me to the door.

My heart was heavy when I turned my back to go out. His voice stopped me though before I could go over the threshold, "By the way, Meg, what would you think if I asked you to go out with me tonight? Would you care for a drink or something later in the evening?" he asked, his tone back to his normal pleasant self as though his momentary outburst hadn't taken place.

For a moment there, I froze. He was offering me exactly what I wanted. That was the moment about which I'd been dreaming since I saw him for the first time.

I looked straight into his eyes to see if he was serious and he was. Nevertheless, I knew it was impossible for me to accept his invitation. It was a real pity.

"I am not sure it is appropriate, Ian…"

"Suit yourself, then!" Ian snapped curtly again and returned to browsing the file he had in his hand.

Suddenly, it was like I had ceased to exist. I was feeling as if I'd been invisible to him and it hurt. I already regretted what I had said but there was no way I could take my words back, especially when, suddenly, the Arctic Ocean made an abrupt appearance between us.

However, I found solace in the fact that it was one day only. Maybe, he would invite me again in the future, and maybe then, I would accept. Everything was open to possibilities.

I don't think I'm strong enough to be able to refuse him again.

Sometimes, boundaries become confused, especially when feelings are involved, and I was afraid that I did have feelings for Ian. Otherwise, I wouldn't have regretted so much that I had to refuse him.

CHAPTER 11

It's strange that, not long ago, I was complaining about being alone all the time yet, when I had a chance to change all that, I simply stepped back, too afraid of the consequences that might unfold. Ian had invited me to go out with him, even if he wasn't interested in me, as a woman. It wasn't something I could be certain about.

However, every time, the same thing happened and I'd always say no. It wasn't the first time I'd done it, but it was the first time I'd refused a man for whom I did have real feelings.

All right, now everything was clear in my mind: I was my own enemy and I'd always ruin all my chances.

Maybe, that was why I was already thirty-four years old and I didn't have a family I could call my own. That was why every evening I returned to an empty and cold house, where there was no one to welcome me and be happy that I was finally back home.

The situation was due to this destructive tendency of mine to step back all the time and, let's be honest here, to that fast track I'd been on since I turned twenty-three. It was as if nothing else had counted in life anymore.

I had to do something about that too if I wanted to also have a full life and not wake up later and see that life had passed me by and I got nothing out of it.

It didn't seem like a problem in the past but things went on and on, and here I was, longing for everything I had missed along my path.

***

I parked my car in the garage next to my cottage and went inside prepared mentally to spend another weekend on my own, reading or watching TV or simply making plans that would never come alive. I was pretty good at making such plans. However, unfortunately, they always vanished before the following day.

I ate some fruit standing in front of the fridge. I was completely famished, and I realized that I hadn't eaten anything since that morning when I had a petty breakfast. I'd actually just nibbled on a muffin on my way to work.

I was in such a bellicose mood that I hadn't felt like eating ever since and I didn't feel any pangs of hunger during the day. I was packed with adrenaline because of my planned meetings.

Now, all that rush was gone and it was like my stomach had been screaming for food for hours and hours and I'd been too deaf to hear it. As a result, I had to pay the price and I had a terrible stomachache.

After finishing my so called dinner, I changed into a comfortable summer dress as the cottage was very good at keeping warmth inside and I could wear light clothes. In the beginning, it seemed strange to see snow outside and feeling like July inside but then I got used to it and I took every opportunity I could.

CHAPTER 12

I was watching a show on TV5 when I heard a car stopping outside suddenly, very close to my house. I could hear the screeching of the brakes and for a moment my heart stopped beating. I expected to hear the loud crash inherent in a car accident, but I heard nothing else but a car door slammed with more force than it would have been necessary.

I wondered if someone had come to visit the people across the street and decided to park their car in my driveway, although I didn't care too much about that. It wasn't as if I'd needed it that night, as no one ever visited me.

Nonetheless, then, I heard the bell ringing and that really puzzled me because I was positive that no one would look for me, especially during that evening. Actually, I had never had a visit there since I came to Paris.

I was aware that there were some people at work who knew where I lived because they had been involved in a way or another in renting and arranging the cottage but they had never come to visit me. It was true that I hadn't even bothered to invite anyone because, besides Ian, the others didn't inspire me any desire to socialize with them.

However, after today's display of power, I wouldn't expect any of my co-workers to ever visit me.

Opening the door, I had the '*real pleasure*' of seeing Philippe, who apparently was in a very special disposition, proven by an unusual shine in his eyes and the uncharacteristic redness of his cheeks. It was obvious that he was in a petulant mood. He was leaning heavily on the door frame, as if he'd been trying to find his balance and keep standing.

Considering his red and turbid eyes, as well as the way he was leaning onto the wall, I could have correctly diagnosed his state – he'd been drinking heavily for at least a couple of hours before coming to visit me so late in the evening. Most likely, the two facts were related, because otherwise I wouldn't have seen Philippe in my neighborhood.

I must admit that I felt a stir of fear inside me but I knew that I couldn't let him see my fear. When you confront a guy in such a bellicose disposition, you'd better not let him see that you were afraid of him because then, you'd be in a real trouble.

"What's the problem, Philippe? Is there some urgent matter at work that couldn't wait till Monday morning or that couldn't be discussed over the phone?" I asked him curtly in a cold voice. I refrained myself from mentioning the fact that he actually wasn't in an appropriate state to discuss business.

Apparently my tone didn't agree with him. He frowned fixing me with his red eyes and a hideous scowl appeared in the corner of his mouth.

Suddenly, he pushed me brutally inside and slammed the door behind him with his foot. As I didn't expect such a move from him, he had no opposition and everything went very smooth for him. The noise of the slamming door resounded in my brain and ears and my heart started beating faster.

I was surprised by the suddenness of his move. I lost my balance and, at the same time, instinctively, a yelp flew off my lips. I couldn't control it.

He appeared to feel happy when he heard me crying out, and he growled his satisfaction. My heart froze instantly because, that very moment, I realized he was willing to go much further than that.

"I knew that you'd want this! I knew that you'd be waiting for this," Philippe hissed through his teeth scornfully. "Like all frigid bitches, you also think only about this!" he said and grabbed my arm. He just kept dragging me after him in the living-room. I tripped and tried to keep standing up. I was pretty sure he'd drag me even if I'd fallen down.

Nevertheless, by the time we got to the living room, I had already passed over my initial shock and I managed to free my arm from his hand with a quick move. Then, I distanced myself from him and I stopped in the middle of the room from where I looked at him angrily. I felt raging hatred rising in my chest.

It was the first time in my life when such a thing had happened to me and I was mad like a cat. Yet, I had to be honest with myself and admit that, up to that moment, I had interacted only with men that had some sense of decorum and dignity. That was why I had always known that a single word would make them leave a room. I was confident that I was safe.

I wasn't so confident about that now, though. I was aware that I didn't have an educated man before me. Philippe had lost his fake shine of civility with one of the many glasses he'd polished that evening. He was a man who had turned into a savage. He didn't care about the consequences of his actions anymore and I was afraid that I would be the one paying for his recklessness.

"I know you are drunk now, Philippe, and I realize that you might have gotten drunk because of your hurt ego, but I advise you to get out of my house right now. If not..."

"If not, what? What could you do to me?" Philippe interrupted me brutally and an ugly smile widened on his lips.

Several times in the past, Philippe had proven to me that he was an individual who lacked essence and character. At the same time, he wasn't a very intelligent man. Now, I could see that he was also sorely lacking in the department of responsibility and consciousness.

Moreover, he seemed to have an innate cruelty which he knew to hide very well when he was sober.

"You have no power over me, Meg. I know very well how you landed this position, keep that in mind. And I also know that you'll do whatever I'd tell you to do after tonight!" he continued sardonically.

His words convinced me that Philippe didn't have any intention to stop there and that I was in a serious trouble, indeed. For a moment I panicked.

I knew to protect myself. That was true. That was something necessary to learn if you lived in New York. You had to learn to defend yourself, especially if you were a woman who lived alone, but so far, I had never been in the situation to apply what I learned.

All of a sudden, I was in unchartered territory and I started to doubt my ability to defend myself against the man I had in front of me. I wasn't even sure that I could remember what I was supposed to do.

Even worse, Philippe might have seemed lean and thin, but I could see his bulging muscles moving under the shirt when he took his coat off and threw it negligently on the floor with a nonchalance that spoke volumes. His gesture indicated he'd made up his mind. It was as if he'd wanted to show to me that there was no way back. I didn't know if he'd really done it to scare me, but I had to admit that the result was exactly that.

For a few seconds, we measured each other, as if we'd been trying to discover the weak points of the opponent, and then, Philippe launched at me. I tried to get away, to pull out of his hands, but he succeeded in grabbing my arms and pulling me towards him.

Now, he didn't seem so unsure on his feet anymore and the lines on his face displayed a strength and resolution of which I hadn't been aware. He'd given me the impression of a weak man who lacked resolution in anything.

I kicked him with my right leg in the shin, and that drove him mad, even though I didn't think that my kick had had too much impact as I was barefoot. In retaliation, he slapped me over the face so hard that I tumbled over the coffee table. On my way down I also brought down with me the tray with my cup of tea and the sugar bowl. I had put them there earlier in the evening and hadn't taken back to the kitchen. The shards from the cup and bowl spread everywhere, powdered with the sugar that had spilled out of the sugar bowl that was now in pieces.

Scared out of my mind, I tried to crawl as far away as possible from him, not paying any attention to the shards that cut my right palm. Nonetheless, even drunk like a skunk and with his faculties inebriated, Philippe proved to be quite fast and he caught me easily. Then he pinned me down on the carpet and tore my summer dress with one brutal pull.

I struggled and tried to scratch him but his forty pounds more made my job extremely difficult if not impossible. I couldn't break free. He bit my neck savagely and the horror of his gesture made me incapable to move for a few seconds and my mind shut down.

It was possible that I fainted for a few seconds because when I came back to my senses, Philippe had already moved down to my chest. The bodice of my dress was in shreds and was hanging over the skirt now, and my bust was completely exposed to his eyes and erring hands.

That made me mad. Furiously, I hit him with all my strength but, unfortunately, the result was not a very happy one for me. It seemed that Philippe believed in paying back tenfold, because he slapped me again and with such an intensity that my teeth chattered. I felt an intense pain on the side of my face and I screamed. I was afraid that he broke my jaw.

I felt his hand on the band of my panties and I thought that I used all my time up. It appeared to be the end of the line, but then, out of nowhere, I saw a big hand pulling his hair and his head was tugged back forcefully.

I finally could catch my breath for the first ever since Philippe had come into my house. With shaking and bloody fingers, I pushed my hair away from my face and looked up just in time to see a big fist striking Philippe strongly in the face. The sound I heard when that fist made contact with Philippe's bones was sickening but it worked. As result, Philippe fell like a log on the floor and, fortunately, he remained there. He was lying down and didn't move anymore.

Looking down at him, almost purple in the face with anger, Ian looked as if he was going to spit on him and tear him into pieces at the same time.

I could say nothing for a few very long seconds and I just waited in the same position on the carpet, watching Ian who seemed to have come out of one of the tapestries depicting knights from the thirteenth or fourteenth century in battle. I had three of them hanging on the walls of my living room.

I noticed immediately when Ian felt my eyes on him. He turned his fiery eyes to me and analyzed me from the top of my head to the tip of my toes, apparently detached, despite the fury that was still simmering in his eyes. I followed his gaze and, to my horror, I realized that I was almost downright naked. My dress was torn behind repair and, with a hurried gesture, I tried to pull the rags around me as quickly as possible, to cover myself somewhat.

Ian shook his head as if he'd thought that my effort was useless and taking my arms, he pulled me up gently.

Now that I was standing up, I realized that I was shaking like a leaf in the wind and I clung onto him to find my balance.

"I really have... to go... and change my ... dress," I said in a shaken voice, which I couldn't recognize, and then I glanced again to what was left of my dress.

I should have stopped calling it a dress now because it was just rags. I also didn't feel comfortable being half naked under Ian's eyes. I was too aware that my state was the result of another man's attack and somehow that shamed me.

Ian nodded understandingly and he let me go but only after he made sure that I had the use of my legs. After he let go of me, he sat down on the sofa and turned to watch Philippe who hadn't come to his senses yet.

I glanced to Ian again. He seemed to be weighing the situation and I thought I'd better let him to it. I wasn't in no shape to do anything right then. Shaking my head, I went on shaken legs towards the stairs.

CHAPTER 13

After I got to my bedroom, I took the liberty to have a long and hot shower. I felt the need to clean my skin of any memory left by Philippe's hands, before getting dressed in a training suit and coming back to the living room where I had left the two men. It was necessary that I had that shower. I couldn't stop shuddering when I was thinking of the way Philippe slobbered all over me and how he touched me.

I was hoping that Ian hadn't beaten Philippe up more in my absence because I didn't want him to get into any trouble because of me.

In my absence, apparently, Philippe had regained his conscience and he was sitting on the sofa now.

From there, he was looking angrily at Ian who, with his hands on his hips, dominated him from the middle of the room. Ian's eyes were as cold as the North Sea in a storm and I effectively shook when I saw the look in his eyes.

"I think you'd better call the police to pick up this piece of garbage immediately," Ian told me without taking his eyes from Philippe even for a second.

It was like he had simply felt my presence in the doorway, because I knew I hadn't made any noise coming down the stairs as I was barefoot.

"I don't know, Ian... It might have a very negative impact on the firm..." I said uncertainly. I didn't know what would be the right thing to do in those conditions.

In normal conditions, of course that I would have called the police. I would have wanted to see Philippe cuffed and if possible thrown into one of the cells in the Bastille. Evidently, I would have even wanted that they'd throw the key into the Seine afterwards.

"I hoped that the company wouldn't matter so much at the moment but I seem to have been wrong..." Ian replied sarcastically. He sounded even disappointed at the same time, and his brutal tone hurt me deeply.

Actually, I knew that he was right. Nevertheless, it was my duty to keep the company out of trouble even if that meant not to punish that piece of garbage. The branch had been recently created and I didn't know if it would have survived the negative comments that would have found their way into the papers.

"You came on time, you know, and he didn't have the time to go too far..." I tried to justify my decision, but Ian cut me off curtly with a wave of his hand.

"It's your decision after all, as you are the harmed party," he said. "But here is my decision now, and if you don't feel comfortable with it, or you think that I should have let you call the shots in such circumstances, it isn't a problem, you'll have your chance to fire me on Monday. Meanwhile," he said heavily turning to Philippe, "I'm still on the job and you are fired right now." Seeing Philippe turning to me, he continued in a steely voice, "And don't look at her because I've also been given the authority to fire employees if I had pertinent reasons, and you know that very well. Keep in mind that I'm the second in charge within the company and I have the right to make decisions when it comes to you. Now get the hell out of here before I come back to my senses and deliver you to the police, as I think I should. If I ever lay my eyes on you again, no matter where and why, I'll show you what real male power is, and believe me, you'll never forget it."

Philippe turned to me, probably thinking that I would contradict Ian, only because it had become a habit of mine and I used to do it so much before. However, this time, I agreed with his decision and to show that I supported him, I got closer to Ian and held my head high.

Philippe swore bitterly and stormed out of my cottage in a fury, slamming the door behind him. It seemed like that was a habit of his, slamming doors. At least where it concerned my doors, that is.

CHAPTER 14

After Philippe stormed out of my house, neither Ian nor I said anything for a few moments. When the silence had stretched for too long and become unbearable, I turned towards Ian, looked straight into his eyes, and said softly, "Thank you, Ian. I thank you from all my heart. Hadn't you come when you came, I don't know what might have happened to me. He was much stronger than I was and I couldn't... couldn't fight him back."

Ian looked at me pensively for a few moments, and then he rubbed his forehead wearily and said, "I heard him in the bar earlier... He was drinking with some friends of his at a table not far from mine. He was speaking quite loud and I overheard him boasting and making plans... At first I thought he was just showing off... You know how he likes to talk big, in general... However, after a while, I thought I'd better make sure that it was nothing more than that, considering what had happened in the afternoon... So I decided to come by and see if you were all right... I should have listened to my instincts and followed him, I know, but usually he seems harmless enough. He likes boasting but he doesn't have too much substance..."

Something in his voice made me sense that he felt guilty about what had happened and I knew he was very wrong. Hadn't it been for him, only God knows in what state I would have been then. I touched his arm gently and told him, "No, Ian, you have already done more than anyone else would have and I am deeply grateful to you for everything."

He shook my hand off his arm with irritation and told me, "I don't need your gratitude! I did only what I thought it was right to do, not because of you especially."

His words hurt me deeply but I tried to smile at him. After all, he was the reason I was still in one piece so I could pass over some rude remarks, even though I would have preferred to hear something else. I would have liked to hear that he cared about me in a special way, that he had done that for me specifically and not because he didn't have it in him to see a woman hurt.

"Would you like something to drink? I surely could use a glass of something strong right now," he said without noticing where my thoughts had wandered. "Is there any whiskey in the house?" Ian continued. "There should be some whiskey because I supplied the drinks among other things when I prepared the house for your arrival and I know for sure that I bought whiskey too. Of course, if you haven't drunk it all by now," he said smiling at me.

"Then, there still is," I answered him and laughed. "I've never verified what kind of bottles are there in the bar since I rarely drink, but if you bought them, then you know better than I do."

"All right, sit there on the sofa and I will prepare the drinks for both of us. I suppose you'd like some ice in yours, wouldn't you?" he asked going to the cabinet to pour the drinks.

"Yes, thank you," I said following his moves with my gaze. He was moving with grace. His gait was springy and that was the proof that Ian was the kind of man that was constantly training to keep himself in a good shape.

I felt safe with him, although, I had never imagined before that I could ever cherish the safety offered by a strong man. I had always been sure that I could count only on my own forces and I hadn't needed a man to make me feel safe. Yet, after the events of that evening, it felt good to know that someone as strong and righteous as Ian was on my side, even though he seemed to be with me only due to some forgotten chivalry norms or due to a misunderstood male sense of duty.

I took the glass he brought to me and wet my lips in the aromatic whiskey. It was not my cup of tea after all, but I knew that its bite might make me feel better. And it did have a bite.

Ian didn't sit down, but kept standing. He kept drinking from his glass and watching out of the window to the snow falling down. The silence stretched, yet it was not an awkward silence. It rather felt good. I was feeling comfortable and at ease with him and I didn't feel the need to speak, to ask him any questions or to make small talk. It was enough that we were together there like that.

"On Monday, I'll present you with my resignation," he said in a calm but rusty voice without turning to me.

Ian startled me and not only because his voice put an end to that contented silence. I was unprepared to hear him speak and, especially, to hear that. I was so shocked that I spilled some of the drink on me. I looked at him with wide eyes as if I couldn't have believed my ears. Actually, at first, I thought I misunderstood what he'd said. It took me a few moments to realize that I had heard him just fine.

"Why? What did I do to you? I don't understand!" I cried out and pushed to my feet. I couldn't stop myself saying that although that was the most idiotic thing I could do.

"Why do you think it is because of you?" he turned towards me, then, with a whimsical smile on his lips.

For a tiny moment there, I forgot the kind of gratitude I owed him. I felt an itch in my palm. I had the urge to erase that smile off his lips with a good slap. I was furious with him because he'd chased away all the illusions I was building in my mind.

In spite of that, I found the strength to stop from lowering myself to my basic instincts, and I raised my eyebrow inquisitively and just stared at him. It was incomprehensible for me. Ian couldn't have believed that I'd have been so air-headed that I couldn't have seen through all that.

"All right, Meg, I admit that it is because of you in a way but it isn't what you think," he said in a rush. "I actually intend to start my own consulting company but, before that, of course, I'll take care to introduce you to a good guy for the adviser position. He's a capable man, with a good portfolio. He'll give you good advice and you'll see that you will be able to trust him."

"But why now? Is it because of the meeting we had in the afternoon? Is it because I insisted on me being the person running the company?" I asked him insistently determined to get some explanations out of him.

"Don't be silly!" Ian snapped at me. "You are supposed to run the firm, obviously. That's why you were sent here. You are actually the boss, and you shouldn't let anyone take that from you," Ian replied to me sternly like he was scolding a child.

I didn't care for his tone too much but I let it pass. At least, he acknowledged that I was in charge and that I should keep that in mind.

"Then... I don't understand what the problem is... really," I said completely puzzled.

"I cannot work with you anymore," Ian confessed. "That's all. What I want from you is something different altogether, Meg, and, unfortunately, it's not compatible with our present positions, boss and subordinate... I'm sure that you see that too. Now, if you want the same thing as I do, it's perfect. If not... Well, I'll survive, it's not a problem. Nevertheless, regardless your decision, I still have to leave the company, Meg. I can't work with you or for you anymore... I hope you understand why...It's too difficult. I do hope you see that," he ended his explanation and there, at the end, there was a pleading nuance in his speech.

I wasn't too sure whether I understood what he was saying or not. I didn't dare to think that, in the end, after so much time and so many nights full of dreams with him in the lead role, his solution would be the answer to all my wishes.

Despite my strong attraction to him, which was proven every night through hot dreams, I had never factored him into the equation, maybe because we were in the positions that he'd already mentioned or maybe because, lately, I had been too furious with him all the time not knowing what to do in order to make a go at it.

Of course, I noticed various things about him, besides his appearance, although I felt tingly every time I saw him, but he really was a damn good-looking guy.

However, it was much more than that. His calm and self-confidence, his intelligence, everything was as attractive as his physical appearance. More than that, he also had brains and empathy, and he seemed to adhere to some of the chivalry notions that had been forgotten along the time.

Afraid of misunderstanding and afraid of starting to make all sorts of plans just to be brought back to earth brutally, I asked him again, "What do you actually mean when you say that you want something else?"

"Oh, God, I don't know how a smart woman like you when it comes to business, could be so stupid when it's about personal relations, Meg!" he said rubbing his forehead anxiously. "Of course, I mean you and me, to be an item. Not at once, obviously. I realize I'd ask too much and too soon but in time, I mean... That's what I want to say. We can start slowly: a dinner here and there, maybe a movie, a play... long walks in Parc des Buttes-Chaumont... You know what I mean."

I looked at him and asked myself why I couldn't have seen this side of him before, his romantic side, because only a romantic guy could think of long walks in a park. Was it because I was too busy imposing myself within the company and too angry with everyone all the time? Was it because of the lack of hope that had seized me during the last few years when I saw myself passing through life alone?

"Good, I see that I've rendered you speechless and overwhelmed with too much enthusiasm for my proposition," he said sarcastically, interrupting the train of thought and thus starting me.

"Nevertheless, keep in mind, no matter what, on Monday you'll have my resignation on your desk. I wish you a good night!" he said in a snippy voice, putting his glass on the little table with more force than necessary and turning to the door to leave.

"Hey, Ian, where are you going?" I jumped off the sofa. "Where's the fire, for God's sake? You jumped to a conclusion and without much support. Who's the ninny now?" I couldn't refrain myself from asking. He scowled at me and I rushed in with an explanation, "You misunderstood my reaction, Ian. Of course, I'm interested in having a relationship with you. I was just woolgathering, that's all. It's just a habit of mine. Maybe it's not the most enticing trait of mine but..." I couldn't continue when I saw his narrowed eyes trained unnervingly on me.

Ian looked at me piercingly to make sure that I was telling the truth and didn't try to sweeten the blow tactfully.

"But I'd also want something more from you, if possible, of course," I decided to continue, even though I felt a sort of hesitation. "I'd also like you to stay here tonight with me, if it doesn't bother you too much... and I mean only to stay...

We drink a little, chat a little…Of course, if you don't already have a hot date in town," I tried to joke, although the thought that Ian would have a hot date made me jealous.

Ian burst into laughter and the room looked instantly as if it were too small for such an outburst. Ian's laugh was strong and full of life. Hearing him laughing so heartily made me feel a little weird, because I didn't know what to think about his attitude. I was somewhat afraid that he had merely made fun of me, prepared to react like that once I had expressed my wishes of building a relationship between the two of us.

He saw me frowning, and pulled me into his arms, whispering to me with his lips in my hair, "Don't worry, baby, I'll be here, today, tomorrow and the day after, if you want me to be here. I'll leave only when you throw me out. Is it all right with you?"

I looked up at him and gazed at him intensely. Ian was really an exceptional sight for my tired eyes.

"Good, then. There's a second bedroom in the house, but you already know that, if I'm not wrong. You can use it," I said pointedly.

"I should have known you wouldn't offer me your bedroom," he replied laughing and, this time, the sound of his laughter warmed its way up into my heart.

CHAPTER 15

Maybe the idea of a relationship with Ian had been in my mind all along, somewhere in the subconscious. There had been little interesting things about Ian that I had noticed unconsciously, but they hadn't found their way to the surface of my mind. He was also my subordinate. That was why I hadn't ever consciously thought of him as a possible partner, because I knew it was an impossible relationship.

However, now, I was able to admit that I had liked him all along and part of my frustration and anger towards him was clearly due to unspoken wishes harbored deeply in my heart.

***

We spent a calm evening together, talking about a lot of things, discovering shared interests and similar points of view about almost everything. We found ourselves on different positions only a few times, but even then the controversy didn't do anything else but make the conversation livelier. The controversy seemed to bring us closer. Having an argument with Ian was an interesting experience.

Time passed unnoticeably and when we realized it was already two o'clock in the morning we couldn't believe our eyes and we burst into laughter like two children that succeeded in finding their way out of curfew.

That was when I showed him to my guest bedroom first – not that I'd ever had a guest until that moment. I knew I shouldn't have bothered because he knew the house but it made me feel better. Then I went into mine, feeling complete and even happy after a very long time.

Not even the evening's events with Philippe bothered me anymore. It was as if they had never happened. I had pushed the thought aside so that I wouldn't ruin the beautiful moments I had had with Ian over the several hours while we talked, cooked a simple dinner together, because I didn't have too many reserves in the fridge, drank a little more but, especially, laughed. We laughed a lot during those first hours spent together.

It was wonderful to laugh so freely, and Ian knew to make everything very funny. He even knew to laugh at himself.

CHAPTER 16

At about six in the morning, I woke up because of the annoying ringing of the phone. I found it difficult to take my arm out from under the comforter, to feel around sleepily to find the receiver and finally answer the phone.

My mind was foggy because I had slept too little. Nonetheless, even in my foggy state, I recognized Mr. Johnson's voice, the big boss from New York. The anger in his voice woke me completely.

I didn't understand what got into him and made him so angry. Yesterday, when I had spoken to him for the last time, everything seemed all right. Moreover, the branch was closed over the weekend, so I couldn't understand what the problem was.

"I want you to come back to New York at once. I don't know what you were thinking, where your mind was, effectively, but I find unbearable the thought that you were able to make such a mess of everything. Here, you seemed a balanced and trustworthy woman and that's why I gave you the promotion but I seem to have been very wrong about you all along. You're not the woman I thought you were!" he thundered.

I was listening to him and I could hear the bite in his words, but I couldn't understand what had happened. I knew him as a wise man, who didn't make any accusations without a solid basis. However, this time I didn't know what his reason was. I was in total darkness.

"I don't understand what could have happened, Mr. Johnson. As far as I know, everything was all right when I left the office yesterday evening, sir," I tried to intervene but he cut me out.

"How could you do it? How could you react like a hysterical little woman? Where was your mind?"

He sounded really hurt and bitter. His voice showed disappointment and that took me aback. I wasn't aware of a single reason for such words. I was sure I didn't deserve to be talked like that as I'd never reacted in any other way but rationally at the office.

"I really don't know what you mean, sir. I really don't. What happened after I left work? No one told me anything."

"Don't tell me you don't know what I am talking about because I'll fire you on the spot without waiting for your return to New York," he barked at me.

"Sir, if you have something to reproach to me, do it, but don't keep acting as if I knew what you were talking about because I absolutely don't know," I replied furiously now.

I wasn't sleepy anymore but I was tired and I felt wronged. I couldn't take his riddles anymore, if they were riddles. I needed him to tell me something straightforward to make a sense of all that nonsense.

"If you want to play this game it's not a problem with me, we can play it," he said sarcastically. "Have you thought that such behavior wouldn't be reported?"

"What behavior, sir?" I asked with my heart in my boots.

"I found out about your habit of constantly harassing the male personnel in the branch! That's what I am talking about!" he almost yelled, losing his temper. "How could you believe that they'd keep quiet, especially after you fired one of them because he didn't answer to your advances?"

"Who are you talking about?" I asked feeling drops of cold sweat running down my spine and on my forehead at the same time.

Now I knew what a real nightmare could be like. It seemed

delusional to think that everything would end like this, based on a lie, but I was too shocked to react as I should have.

"I'm talking about Philippe, of course! He called me this morning to tell me everything."

"Really?" I replied sardonic at my turn, more alert now. "Did he also tell you about how he attacked me last night and tore my clothes off? Did he tell you how he came into my house and tried to rape me?"

"I'm sorry, but I can't believe you. He has a witness concerning the harassment and I was told you threatened to fire her too if she didn't keep her mouth shut."

"Yes, it was Mireille probably," I replied calmly. The worse had already passed and I felt strangely calm. "It's true, I told her that I'd fire her but not if she didn't keep her mouth shut about a fantasy. I told her she'd be fired if she didn't start pulling her weight because up to now she hasn't done anything. So, this is your witness…"

"Unfortunately for you, they're two and they're very persuasive. I believe them, and that's it. Both of them sounded sincere and I have to protect this firm against any civil suit. I had to offer a raise to both of them to make them want to remain with the company and now, I have to call you back to New York. I can't let you there anymore. I'll give you the benefit of the doubt and maybe, back on familiar ground, you'll react less wretchedly for yourself and the company. I hope you realize that I do this as a favor to you and only because you worked with us for so long. Otherwise, I would have fired you at once."

I didn't say anything for a few moments and I took the time to analyze the situation. Suddenly, I knew what I wanted to do.

"Mr. Johnson, I'll not come back to New York anyway, and it's not necessary to fire me. I'll send you my resignation by email right away, probably within half an hour. I am sorry of course that you don't know all the facts and that the branch here will really go down from now on, but this isn't my problem anymore so..."

"What are you going to do there?" he replied seeming bewildered.

He probably couldn't believe that I was about to throw all the years during which I worked within his company out the window. It had been over a decade.

"Live, sir, just live," I replied to him coldly. "Please, don't bother to show me any concern now, because it doesn't matter anymore. You've shown no concern when I told you that I was almost raped by one of your employees, so don't bother to do it now. I don't care about your concern now. I think you shouldn't bother with me anymore now, either," I continued always sarcastically, as he deserved it.

"Listen, Meg, it's not as if…"

"It isn't, but my decision is made," I cut him off. "It's not a problem, Mr. Johnson. I'm just sorry that the branch for which I worked so hard is in such a precarious position now, but you made your choice and soon the results will be seen. It's not like it's my company, so... I have only one question for you: do you want to keep the cottage for the next person that you'll send here to run the company?"

"I won't send anyone there anymore. I'll appoint Ian or Philippe at the direction of the company so I won't need that cottage anymore. Of course, I'll have to do something with the contract we signed but ..."

"I'd like to take over the contract myself if it isn't a problem," I interrupted him. "Could you discuss this matter with the realty agent and make it happen at the beginning of the week? As a favor for all the hard work I've done for your company for over a decade, as you've already mentioned," I told him businesslike.

"Yes, of course, I can do that, but do you have the means to keep it?" he wondered at my request.

"This is only my business, Mr. Johnson," I said more abruptly than I'd have wanted but there was too much cold inside me at that moment to sound more charming and tactful.

Apparently he felt that there was a change in my voice because he changed the subject abruptly:

"On Monday morning, you have the time to take all your personal things from your office. I'll make all the announcements on Tuesday so that your replacement could take over things before Christmas."

"It works for me, sir. You can do it sooner, actually. On Monday at nine I'll gather my things. It's not like I have too many personal things in the office. It won't take me more than an hour so you can make your announcements immediately after ten."

"No, it's no rush. On Tuesday, it's soon enough," he said conciliatorily.

"Suit yourself," I replied, always cold. "It's the same thing for me, anyway. Then, I'll tell you goodbye, sir, and in approximately thirty minutes you'll have my resignation in your email."

"Good! A good day then, Meg!" he replied curtly and, finally, rang off.

I tried to say something along the same line but there was no one on the line anymore, and I wasn't too sorry that I was spared expressing something I didn't feel. I got out of bed at once. I was awake now and, anyway, I didn't have time to waste in bed if I wanted to end all my business with the company in half an hour.

I took a long shower to clear my thoughts a little and to analyze my decision of leaving everything I knew behind in order to start all over again from the beginning. It seemed like a good decision in the heat of the moment.

Sometimes, I was impulsive – a habit I had been trying to temper all my life. Nonetheless, now, I had some fears. The situation was what it was and being afraid wasn't too out of ordinary.

I knew that I had the financial means to survive for a few months, probably, half a year, after I'd paid the rent for the cottage, but nothing more. I had to find something to do and soon, if I didn't want to sell the house in New York.

I went downstairs and I prepared the coffee maker because I needed some coffee. Waiting for the coffee to be ready, I decided to turn my computer on and start writing my resignation letter.

I felt a sort of regret, to be true. It would have been hard not to feel anything because I had worked for this company from the beginning of my career, immediately after leaving the university. At that time, I had started a long and hard road, as an intern first. Then, I kept being promoted step by step until I landed here in Paris.

My entire adult life, or almost all of it, I'd known nothing else but working with the same company. I had given them my best years and that was why I was feeling betrayed in the end. It was no wonder, after all. I felt duped, because, actually, the bad guy had won and with one deed had effectively taken away everything I had worked for, all the days and nights of hard work that no one could give back to me now. The injustice made me feel rancorous and I was sure that feeling would stay with me for a long time.

The noise of the coffee maker made me come back to the real world and taking my eyes from the computer screen, where I had written only one line by now, I noticed Ian, who had come downstairs.

I hadn't even heard his steps on the stairs, as I was deep in my thoughts. He was leaning on the door frame, his arms crossed over his chest and he was looking at me thoughtfully. His grey eyes had that enigmatic light, always the same, which every single time I saw it made the butterflies in my belly dance. Evidently, even now, I felt a strange heat invading my face.

I couldn't read his thoughts and, besides that, his body language was so baffling that I couldn't make anything of it. It felt like I was trapped in an unfamiliar situation and, as result, I didn't know what to do or what to say.

For a few long minutes, we watched each other and then Ian came towards me, keeping his eyes intensely focused on mine all the time, making me feel as if I'd been the only woman in the world that mattered to him. Then, he pulled me to my feet and towards him quite unexpectedly. He held me tightly in his arms as if he hadn't wanted to let me go ever again. This simple gesture made me feel that I'd finally got home after a road that seemed endless.

I didn't know if he had overheard the conversation I had earlier. It seemed impossible, but he seemed to know that something was very wrong with me and I felt relieved that I didn't have to tell him that I needed to be held.

I'd never been able to ask for anything, but especially to ask someone to soothe me. I could never find the right words to ask someone to comfort me. I had learned to rely only on myself in any kind of situation, but it seemed that now, I could lean on someone else, and that made me happy.

He held me silently for a while, leaning his forehead to the crown of my head, in silence. Only after a while he told me gently, "I'll pour you a cup of coffee now. I think you need it after so little sleep last night. Make yourself comfortable meanwhile, Meg."

I would have loved to lie down on the sofa and wait for him to fetch my coffee to me. I didn't recall anyone ever bringing me coffee in the morning up to now, or if they had, that had happened so far in the past that I couldn't even remember. I would have savored his thoughtful gesture, but, unfortunately, I had to finish my resignation letter and send it because I was getting close to the end of the thirty-minute window.

I decided to keep it as short as possible and I wrote it in the most neutral tone that I could muster. I didn't find that it was necessary to go into details or to express any regret or disappointment.

When I pushed the send button, I had the acute feeling that my life was flowing away through my fingers, all those years spent in meetings that seemed endless, or trying to conclude the most profitable business in order to have the best performance within the team.

CHAPTER 17

An important chapter in my life ended then and there when I clicked SEND. I must confess that my finger shook on the mouse when I did it.

I embraced myself to numb somewhat the shock I felt at the thought that a long episode in my life had ended, and then, I closed my eyes because the light of dawn was hurting my eyes. It poured a diffuse pain in my heart. I felt tears under my eyelids but I refused to let them fall.

I opened my eyes only when the smell of coffee had become so strong that it meant that a cup of coffee was held right under my nose. I could feel the steam tickling my nose.

I was a bit bothered by Ian's manner of walking without making the slightest noise and I opened my mouth to say something about it, only to shut it almost immediately. I didn't think that you could reproach someone for having a catlike gait unless they used that skill to harm you, and so far, Ian had proved exactly the opposite. He was by my side in the toughest moments of my life and maybe, hadn't it been for him, I couldn't have found the strength to go on.

I smiled at him and took my cup of coffee from his stretched hand. I sipped the aromatic and hot liquid that Ian had sweetened to my taste. He seemed to have remembered how I liked my coffee because he had added the perfect quantity of sugar and milk. I felt a little better, as if I'd been myself again. That meant that I was on the right path and coming back to my normal self.

"Can you tell me what's happened this morning?" he asked me showing me to the sofa.

I looked at him for a few instants, and I sipped some more coffee just to gain more time. I didn't know how to start my story. Then, lit one of the four cigarettes I used to smoke every day. Only afterwards, I told him about the phone call that had woken me up that day and everything that unfolded afterwards.

"I knew it, Meg. I knew that it would be like that!" he said bitterly clenching his fists furiously. "I told you to call the police last night, Meg, but you refused because you were stubbornly thinking only about the reputation of the firm. I hope you're happy now because it seems that the company forgot to show you the same consideration in return."

"I know I made a mistake and that you were right, Ian. I don't think that you should rub my nose in..."

"I'm sorry, if I have given you the impression that I was doing that," he interrupted me. "It wasn't my intention, baby. Anyway, what happened, happened, we can't turn the time back, so we'd better focus on the future. So, what are you going to do now?"

"I've already sent my resignation by email," I told him and saw him scowling. "I couldn't have worked there anymore, Ian", I rushed to tell him. "Moreover, they had asked me to come back to New York, and, for the moment, I don't have anything there. Nothing good, you know. Here, at least, I can try and make a new life for myself… and maybe I could build a relationship with you… of course, if you still want the same thing, no matter how short you might want that relationship…" I was aware I was lost coherence in my speech but I was afraid he'd think that I assumed too much.

"Not very short, love! Not very short!" he said taking my hand and kissing it. "You know what Meg? Let's have breakfast first of all. I am the type of guy that needs a huge breakfast first thing in the morning. I can't do without. If I don't have it, I can get quite morose. We have to go out though, I'm afraid, because we

135

already finished what you had in the fridge last night."

I burst into laughter although I knew that he was somewhat serious. Nonetheless, the same time, the utterance of such a mundane matter in the middle of a conversation like that, made me feel like I were breaking free, as if any burdens I had before just vanished in thin air.

He raised his eyebrow curiously but didn't say anything, although he kept looking after me when I left the room to get dressed. I was still laughing but I could still feel the caress of his eyes over the skin of my back.

There was an entire nervous load piled up inside me and that needed to find a way out somehow. Laughing didn't seem like such a bad idea.

Getting dressed for the weather outside because it had started snowing again, and it seemed to be a little windy, my thoughts wandered on their own.

I was aware that I had chosen a new path, yes, unknown and a bit frightening, if I had to analyze things carefully, but that might turn out being quite rewarding in the end. I had followed a straight road up until a few months ago, and I had felt trapped in a cage, in a world that wasn't for me anymore. I'd stopped enjoying it enough because I didn't have any satisfaction. Everything had become just a chore, both my job and the necessity of interacting with some people…

Suddenly, I realized that choosing a new path at a crossroads might give you a chance and help you feel that life had a new meaning, that you were alive. There was the possibility to find fulfillment and feel enthusiastic for something again.

Going down the stairs, I saw Ian in the doorway, his coat in his hand already. What I saw in his eyes was more meaningful to me than anything else lately. It felt like he was my future – uncertain, that was true, maybe stormy, that was also true, considering both of our tempers, but it was real and solid the same time, full of the promise of new beginnings.

When we locked the door behind us, I felt like I had left my boring past behind that door and walked forward on a new path open wide in front of me, full of promises. Maybe what I was thinking was outdated, but for the moment, I didn't care about that. I had spent enough time to keep up with the times and requirements. It was the moment to digress a little and live just for myself.

CHAPTER 18

Ian took my hand and pulled me after him, going round the car he had left on my driveway the night before.

"Aren't we taking the car?" I asked him.

"Not now. Maybe later. I know for sure that there is a little café right around the corner and we can have breakfast there. I know from experience that they bake awesome buns and also serve an omelet with everything. They even make those little sausages for breakfast if you want some. Their pastries are absolutely delicious. I had the chance to taste some fantastic croissants there. They simply melt in your mouth, you'll see. Right next to the café, there are some small neighborhood shops where we can find everything we need for today or tomorrow. I don't understand why you don't know more about your neighborhood," Ian wondered.

"I haven't really had time to visit the neighborhood, Ian. Generally, whenever I needed something, I just checked on-line to find a supermarket or a specific store," I replied to him shrugging.

"Yeah, too much work and too little play! I know how you usually spend your day, kitten, and believe me, you need a change. You see, that's what you need, to get rid of this hellish rhythm you've indulged in for a long time."

I smiled to him but I wasn't really in the mood. I knew he was right and that I had to start relaxing a little more. I had passed through a very tense period and I could physically feel it. The muscles in my neck and shoulders were so tense that the pain had become a constant companion to me. It would have been an excellent idea if Ian offered to give me a massage. I was sure his strong hands could work wonders on my tortured muscles.

"Of course, if you want, tonight we can go out to a restaurant and maybe we could go to a movie later on…" Ian said putting his arm around my shoulders and pulling me closer to him.

"What about… if I wanted that we'd stay at home, prepare dinner together again and maybe watch one of the movies that someone took care to provide me with, so generously?" I asked him playfully.

"Better that way," Ian replied to me smiling. "It's exactly what I'd love best. Meg, you know, I want us to spend as much time together as possible, to give you the chance to get to know me… I know everything that's important about you, and the rest will come in time. You never can know everything about someone, and that would be too dull in the end, wouldn't it? There would be surprises, nothing new to discover… But I want you to be sure…"

I looked up at him, gazed at him for a few moments in silence, and then I said, "I know what I want, Ian, and what we have between the two of us right now sounds perfect. It's exactly what I want... Ian, you should know that I've arranged to have the leasing contract transferred to my name so that I could stay here, in this house. I'd like it if you'd spend more time with me, here, in my house..."

"Not a problem," he laughed. "It's exactly what I've planned", he added, gathering me tightly to him.

CHAPTER 19

We ordered a copious breakfast at the counter and then retreated to a small table that Ian chose. It was out of the path in a corner of the café. I was delighted with his choice, because I wanted to be able to talk to him without being afraid of anybody's curios ears.

"I also got a call from Mr. Johnson, when you went upstairs to get dressed," Ian told me, taking my hand and gazing at me affectionately, after we took our seats at the table.

I felt a little stab in my heart again, but, after all, it didn't really matter anymore. The past was in the past. It was gone. I shouldn't have thought of it anymore.

"What did he want to tell you?" I asked him softly. I didn't really want to hear his answer.

Ian caressed my hand gently, and then squeezed my fingers affectionately. A moment later, he turned my palm up and he kissed it right in the center.

"He wanted to offer me your position. Of course, he started the conversation presenting first his apologies for what I had possibly suffered because of your behavior. It was really interesting to hear what he had to say about that."

I frowned furiously. I was deeply ashamed and hurt because the lies that Philippe had spread were already considered absolute truth.

"Don't frown, kitten, it's not worth it. Anyway, I also told Mr. Johnson what I needed to say. I explained to him what I thought about your behavior during the entire period you were in charge here at the branch and then I told him that not only I couldn't accept the position he offered to me, but I couldn't even conceive to continue to work for a company that rewarded hard work and dedication with unfounded accusations, as they'd done with you. I told him that he hadn't even thought to verify first if what that garbage, Philippe, told him was real and only then, if it was true, to start throwing stones. I made it clear that I found that inadmissible."

By the end of his speech, Ian had really girded himself. He was mad and his expression was ferocious. It was clear that he wasn't a man one wanted to cross if they didn't want to find out what he was able to do.

"And what did he say to all that?" I asked curious.

"He was extremely surprised about what I said and told me that he had to re-evaluate the situation in that case. I replied to him that he could do whatever he wanted, but he shouldn't count on me working for him anymore after he'd treated you the way he did. He didn't even take into consideration what you told him about the fact that you'd been about to be raped. He hadn't thought of what you'd gone through, not for one single moment..." Ian said, and then he touched my right cheek that was badly swollen and sported a horrible bruise. "I presented him with my resignation on the phone, and then I also sent him a brief email from my phone, you know, to be completely covered... You know what, Meg? I think he'll call you again, maybe to apologize to you or maybe to offer you your job back..."

"He can call, Ian, I don't care. I'm not interested in working for the company anymore, you know that."

Ian gazed at me lingeringly, as if he wanted to make sure that I was telling the truth, and then he asked me, "What do you think about working with me? I know what they say that it's not a good idea for a couple to work together but... honestly, I don't think it would be a problem, at least not for me... Don't say anything now, just think about it. Of course, I know that there's also the possibility that you might want to work in a completely different field altogether or take a longer vacation... and truth be told, you're due for a vacation, I think."

I looked back at him for a few long moments without saying anything. It wasn't as if I hadn't wanted to work with him. I knew what kind of man he was and how he approached work. I wasn't even afraid of controversies, especially because I knew for sure that when it came to work, he was extremely calm, and he would have balanced things, complimenting my personality. However, I felt the impulse of trying something else, something I had been thinking about for a long time but I had always put the idea aside as being unrealistic.

"You know, it's been a while that I've been thinking of trying something and I haven't had either the time or the courage to do it..."

"What would you want to do?" Ian asked me, taking my hand in his huge palm again.

He seemed to need to be in contact with me all the time and that not only flattered me, but it was something I really liked. I looked at our joined hands, mine completely lost in his palm, and I felt that, finally, everything was exactly as it should be. This was the place where I had to be, together with this man, who up to this moment succeeded in proving to me that I wasn't taking second place in his life. That was something no one ever proved to me in my lifetime.

"Maybe you'd laugh at me..." I started shyly and then stopped.

Ian burst into laughter, squeezed my fingers gently and then said, "I think that the only thing that might make me laugh at you is if you'd tell me that you decided to play professional basketball, not for any other reason but you are very small, and you have no chance there. In my opinion, Meg, you have all chances to succeed in anything else. You have the willpower you need in order to succeed. I know you're intelligent and you have the vision you need to accomplish anything you try."

"First wait to hear what I have to say," I told him, and, slapped his hand playfully.

"All right, I'm listening to you, Meg. What do you want to do?"

I didn't get to say anything because the waitress came with the food and I pulled my hand back from his to make room for her to put the plates and cups on the table.

Only after she left, I tilted my head towards him, as if I were afraid that someone could hear me, and I told Ian in secret, "I always wanted to write books for children, with fantastic stories or legends…"

Ian remained engrossed in thought for a few moments, and then asked me, "Well, what stops you from doing that now? I think you can take a little time off, at least until you finish writing the first book, and then, we'll see what will be. It's not like you have to start a new job first thing Monday morning. If we are to build a relationship between the two of us, kitten, then I understand that you should rely on me for a period of time at least, although I'm thinking of something long term."

"Oh, that's not a problem. I can manage financially, no worries. In principle, I'm covered with the expenses for about six months, even if I don't make any money and I don't touch my investments portfolio to sell some of the shares I have. I think that in six months, I'll know one way or another how far I can get with my writing, if it is something for the future or not."

I searched his face with my eyes to see what he was thinking about that, but, as it had happened whenever we were talking shop, I couldn't read anything in his expression. He had the talent to show a completely expressionless face to his opponent.

"I say you should do it," he finally said. "Whether you support yourself financially or you let me help you, for me is the same thing, although, truth be told, I think that I'd have preferred to know that you trusted me enough to support you."

"But I am, that's not the problem here. Nonetheless, I'd like to succeed through my own forces, you know. Anyway, if you are determined to continue with what is between us two, you can move in with me, and then it would be like you'd contribute to my keep as well."

"Yeah, you're tactful, like always, but you can't fool me, Meg."

"What do you mean? Don't you want to live with me? No problem! I'm sorry if I misunderstood you, Ian," I snapped at him.

I was totally confused and I didn't find he was too honest right then. Up to now, he had kept saying that he wanted a relationship with me, and when I metaphorically offered him the keys to my house, he simply did a one-eighty.

"Calm down, Meg, calm down! Don't jump to conclusions so fast! I was just saying that you threw me a little bone so that I wouldn't feel neglected, when in fact you have no intention to let me contribute to your keep. I didn't even think of saying that I didn't want to live with you. After all, it's what I want the most... I'll have to see what I can do with the flat that I have leased, but I'm not worried about it. There are enough people who want to lease it, so I can solve it in a few days... Of course, I'd like if we'd start living together from now on," Ian said and started eating heartily, as if everything had already been concluded and it wasn't necessary to discuss the subject anymore.

It was a real pleasure to see him eating. He didn't seem to make any effort, but the food vanished off his plate fast. More bizarre was the fact that I didn't know where all that food was going, because even though he was a bear of a man, no one could say that he was fat.

Ian saw me watching him without eating and looked at me inquiringly, his eyebrow going up - a gesture that makes him look much more interesting. I smiled and bit into a butter croissant to show him that I hadn't forgotten about the food in front of me.

"You know what I think?" Ian asked me between two bites.

I copied his move with the eyebrow and he burst into laughter, effectively spraying me with the coffee he was just drinking. He jumped up and yanked a few napkins from the napkin holder to clean me, "I'm sorry, Meg! Don't make me laugh when I drink something!" he said cleaning my face with a napkin.

Unfortunately, his zeal was more than my hurt cheek could stand and I cried out, "Ouch! It hurts!"

I saw the playful light in his eyes turn into a metallic shine. Apparently, I reminded him of what had happened the night before and it was exactly what I didn't want. I wanted him to forget completely about it and we could feel good together without having the phantom of the other night's attack between us. I touched the back of his hand and said softly, "You know it's not your fault, don't you? Let's not think of that anymore, Ian. I am sure that we could find something more interesting to talk about or do."

Ian nodded affirmatively, although a little hesitant, and then he intertwined his fingers with mine, and pensively, he stared at our hands.

"I know this is a question everybody hates, Ian, but I have to ask it. What are you thinking about?"

Ian looked up at me. A smile appeared on his lips and then, gradually, the smile reached his eyes as well. He pulled my hand playfully, and then he said, "It seems I succeeded to make my way into your house. Now, I wonder if I also won a spot in your bedroom too or if

I have to content myself with the same room I had last night."

His question caught me unaware. I hadn't thought so far, but actually, I hadn't even thought that I had to consider that too. If I had invited him to live with me, my subconscious had already accepted the idea that we'd share the bed together.

I didn't answer aloud, but I nodded briefly, expressing my agreement silently. I also felt that my face had turned red, and I realized then that he'd already noticed my blush. Now, he was very amused by my reactions. I slapped his hand lightly – I was feeling too embarrassed to admonish him verbally.

Ian laughed heartily, and then he touched the tip of my nose teasingly.

"I think that it's clear that now I can't wait to get home. Even going shopping seems like a waste of time," he told me.

I felt I was getting redder, but at the same time a peculiar heat spread all over inside my body and the butterflies in my belly came alive. Only just to be against his idea, because I wanted to have the necessary time to get back to normal, I said, "No, first we do the groceries and then we go home. I don't want to see you limp around later because you didn't have anything available to recharge your energy."

Only when I saw how astonished he was and when he burst into loud laughter, I realized what he could have understood from what I said and I couldn't find anything else to do but to cover my eyes mortified. My gesture made him laugh even louder and I uncovered my eyes and gave him a dark glance. Then, I also discovered that all the customers in the coffee shop turned their eyes to us.

"What's so amusing?" I hissed at him.

"Calm down, kitten, calm down," he said. "There's no need to take out your little claws. You were funny, so it was normal to laugh, but

I assure you that I wasn't laughing at you. Nonetheless, you must admit that the double entendre of what you said was hilarious," he tried to cajole me.

It was funny, indeed, and I burst into laughter as well. That seemed to please him immensely.

"Let's pay and leave," he said. "I feel like I have no patience to do the groceries and we need to get it over with it soon. I think that you are aware that you've played an important role in my fantasies for a long time," he continued waving in the general direction of the waitress, because in fact he kept gazing at me with hungry eyes.

His hungry gaze made me feel antsy and now, I was sorry I had insisted to go shopping first. I was sure we wouldn't have starved to death if we had waited to do our shopping for a few more hours. The promises I could read on Ian's face were much more than I could stand and I felt my skin tingling. The wait had become unbearable.

Ian took out money from his wallet to pay when the waitress finally came with the bill, and I was ready just to stand up and put the coat on. Exactly when I was thinking that we could go out of the coffee shop and start our race against the clock, so that we could get back to the comfort of my house where we could do something to soothe those butterflies in my belly that were extremely active, the phone I had left in the pocket of my winter coat rang.

Ian looked at me warily, and I shrugged my shoulders taking out the phone and glancing at the screen.

"It's Mr. Johnson," I told Ian in answer to the question which I read in his eyes.

"Are you going to answer?"

"Honestly, I don't know if it makes any sense to answer," I replied, torn between the need to hear what my former boss had to say and the desire to never hear his voice again.

"Maybe, you'd better hear what he has to say," Ian advised me.

I thought about it a few more seconds, but then I decided that he was right and I answered the phone.

"Hello, Meg speaking."

"I'm glad you answered my call, Meg," Mr. Johnson said. "It's necessary that I apologize for talking to you earlier in such an outrageous way. You were right when you said that I didn't have all the details and I simply relied on the words of those two individuals. No worries, I'll take care of them from now on."

I didn't know what to reply. I felt relieved that he knew the truth now and he wasn't left with that awful impression about me. Nonetheless, it seemed like too much to be asked to forget the horrible things he had told me in the morning.

"Are you there, Meg?" he asked me when I didn't give him an answer.

"Yes, Mr. Johnson, I'm still here. I'm glad that you found out the truth in the end and you stopped considering me some sort of femme fatale who ruined your company with her slutty behavior," I replied sharply.

For a few heartbeats, silence reigned on the line, and then I heard his voice again.

"I think I deserve these words, Meg. I should have listened to my better judgment. It was telling me insistently that a person that you'd known for over a decade couldn't change completely overnight. I know you are extremely upset and, probably, very hurt right now, but I'd like you to reconsider your resignation and remain at the management of the branch in Paris. Evidently, you'll also get a raise and your yearly bonus for this year will be twenty percent higher than we have decided before."

I didn't answer him but I looked at Ian. His face told me that he was aware of what I was offered, but he didn't try to push me towards any specific decision. He let me decide for myself. I appreciated his confidence in my abilities, and the fact that he knew that I could make the best decision.

I understood more than ever that Ian was the quintessence of my future, and that my future had to be completely separated from my past. I had to give myself the chance to achieve what I wanted, and Ian was what I wanted. Nevertheless, I also wanted that my life took a completely different direction than the one I had had until now. Only then, I would have felt fulfilled.

"I appreciate your offer, Mr. Johnson, but my decision remains the same. This is not only because if I accepted your offer, it would mean to live in fear from now on. I'd fear that I might make a decision related to one of the employees and knowing that if the respective employee contacts you with an aberrant story, you'd believe it immediately, no questions asked. However, this is not my only reason. I want to have the possibility to decide the evolution of my career from now on, without having to report to anyone else. So, no, I can't accept your offer, and my resignation still stands."

Ian took my hand, squeezed my fingers hard, so hard that it almost hurt, and then he tilted his head to me and kissed my lips lightly.

I have to say that all my fantasies about that mouth that was so beautifully sculpted didn't do it real justice. What I felt in reality was much more intense, much better than in any of my dreams. If I felt like that when he didn't do anything more than touching his lips to mine, then a real kiss would have certainly short-circuited my mind completely.

"Meg, I'm sure you are too upset and hurt right now to think clearly," I heard Mr. Johnson's voice coming as if from far away. "Maybe, it's better to take a day or two, Meg, to think things over and then give me your final answer," he continued.

"It's not necessary, Mr. Johnson, because my answer will not change at all tomorrow or even after a month. I'd better tell you this now, so that you could find someone competent for the management of the company in due time. You shouldn't have any illusions about my coming back to work for the company."

I could hear him grinding his teeth angrily but he didn't say anything for a few seconds and I waited patiently to see what more he wanted to say.

"All right," he finally said. "I see that I have no other choice but to accept your decision. Could you at least stay at the management of the branch until after New Year's Eve, until the fifth of January? So that we could find someone else to take your position?"

I thought about it for a few moments and I was tempted to say no, but he continued in a rush so that I hadn't had the time to decline his offer on the spot, "Of course, that means that I'll pay you double for the next following weeks, and you will also get a higher bonus," he tried to persuade me.

It was tempting, especially knowing that the bonus he was talking about would help me live comfortably for a while. I glanced at Ian but I saw that he kept a neutral air, as if he hadn't wanted to influence me at all.

"All right," I replied, "I'll be in charge until after the New Year, but no more. Whether you succeed in finding a replacement or not, I won't stay any longer, my resignation remains the same, just the date changes. And of course, I want that bonus transferred into my account Monday morning."

"I understand that you don't trust me anymore," my boss said with sadness.

"It would be absurd to trust you anymore, sir, don't you think? Only this morning you showed me that you could change your mind from a moment to another, in the blink of an eye. So, I need some insurance." I replied coldly.

He didn't answer immediately. He seemed to think about it, and then he said, "I'll take care of the transfer to your account now. On Monday, you'll have the money for the bonus as well as the total of your compensation that should be paid to you until the fifth of January. But you stay on the job until the fifth of January, Meg," he specified.

"Not a problem, Mr. Johnson. Until now, I've always done what I said, and I haven't ever given you a reason to doubt me," I replied cynically, knowing he'd get the reference.

"Well, that's true," he muttered. "All right, so we leave it at that. Maybe you'll manage to convince the Irishman to stay until the beginning of the year too, so that we could find a replacement for him as well... On Monday, you'll have the money in your account and you continue to do business as usual until the fifth of January. Then, we speak next week," he ended the conversation suddenly, and, as usual, he hung up without giving me a chance to say anything more.

Ian was gazing at me inquiringly because, apparently, I had looked suddenly at him when I heard that I had to persuade him to stay until the beginning of the year. I avoided his eyes for a few moments, and then, I started playing with the belt at my winter coat to gain some time.

"What else did he want from you? I can see that you hesitate to tell me," Ian asked me softly, raising my head with a finger under my chin.

"Not much, really," I replied shyly. "He wants me to work for the company until the fifth of January, so that he has time to find someone else and…"

"And what?" he insisted seeing my hesitance.

"Well, he wants me to convince you to stay with the firm at least until then so that he could find someone to take your place."

"I see," he said. "And how do you intend to persuade me?" he asked me teasingly.

"I don't know, maybe I'll just ask you if you wanted to stay…"

"Hmmm, you aren't very persuasive, really," he joked and playful lights shone in his eyes. "I think you have to find something else to persuade me with. I'm not so easy when it comes to changing my mind."

"Really? And if I ask you nicely?" I asked him and fluttered my eyelashes to him, as the divas of the sixties used to do.

He went into shrieks of laughter, caught me in a bear embrace that made me almost lose my breath, and then he said, "Consider that you've already convinced me!"

I tapped on his arm to make him understand that I wanted him to release me, and when I saw that he didn't get it, I elbowed him strongly and said out of breath, "I can't breathe, Ian!"

Alarmed, he let go of me quickly and asked me anxiously, "Are you all right? I didn't realize…"

"Not a problem," I said after I took a deep breath. "It seems that you are not truly aware of your strength, Ian."

"I'm sorry, baby. I'll try to remember from now on that you are small and delicate. But you're all right now, aren't you?"

I nodded affirmatively and put my gloves on. Then I took his hand and we left the coffee shop in a hurry. We both wanted to finish with the shopping faster so that we could return home sooner.

CHAPTER 20

No sooner had we put the bags on the kitchen table, that Ian pulled me towards him and took my mouth in a kiss that erased everything else from my mind. I clung to him so that I could keep my balance but I still had the impression that I was totally melting in his arms. It felt like I was somewhere in the middle of a hurricane. All my senses had come to life at once and I couldn't make any distinction between one sensation and another.

Ian stopped for a moment, kissed my lips again, lightly, then he kissed the tip of my nose and squeezed me to his chest.

"You have too many clothes on you," he whispered into my ear, and his hot breath made me shiver.

It seemed too much at the same time. Generally, in such circumstances, my mind would wander to other things, but this time, I was completely lost in him. Sensations overwhelmed me from everywhere and bombarded my system ruthlessly, abandoning me to his mercy.

"Let's take our winter coats off and go upstairs. We can take care of the rest afterwards."

His words brought me back to reality and I glanced towards the bags on the table.

"I'm afraid that there are some things in there that should be put in the fridge as soon as possible," I replied to him uncertainly turning to face him again.

"My practical little kitten!" he muttered, and taking off his winter coat threw it on one of the chairs.

"You know what? I'll take care of all of these, and meanwhile, you go upstairs, make yourself comfortable and wait for me. I'll be there soon. It won't take me more than a few minutes to take everything out of the bags and put them into the fridge or cupboards."

For a few moments, I hesitated but I felt a shiver that reminded me of what he had awoken in my body with only one kiss, so I took his winter coat off the chair, and turned to the hall to leave it in the wardrobe together with mine. Afterwards, I went upstairs to the bedroom, where I took my boots off first, and then I my sweater and pants.

I remained in the middle of the room for a few seconds. I didn't know what more I should do. I wasn't sure whether he expected me to take off every single stich of cloth or not, but I didn't feel at ease to wait for him completely naked.

I was still deliberating what to do when I heard him coming upstairs and I just froze. Now, I absolutely didn't know what to do anymore.

Ian appeared in the doorway and took a good look at me, his eyes covering every inch of my body lazily. I had only my panties and bra on, and I congratulated myself that I had chosen a sexier set that morning at least.

With his catlike gait, he came slowly to me, took my cheek into his palm, and gazed deeply into my eyes. Then, he angled his head and his lips stopped just a split second away from mine. I could feel the heat of his lips and his light breath. Shyly, I put my hand on his own, sliding it up, mapping out the contour of his arm, heading slowly towards his shoulder, burrowing my fingers into the muscles that were flexing under my touch. When I got to his neck, I stroked him gently, and then I pulled him towards me, impatient to feel the texture of his lips again.

Ian laughed softly, amused by my boldness, but then any kind of amusement disappeared from his eyes. He became intent and pulled me almost savagely towards him with his right arm, and his left palm tilted my head so that he could fit his lips onto mine better. He tasted each of my lips, separately, with a sense of urgency that made me dizzy. I felt his teeth biting my lower lip, and then I felt his tongue wetly soothing the sting of his bite. Then, his tongue slid over mine, dueled with it, and stole any coherent thought I had had in my head.

I felt his palm drifting towards my neck slowly, searchingly, stroking me and arousing thousands of sharp sensations that I could feel even in the lower part of my body. I breathed deeply and I inhaled his musky scent, which reminded me of how good his rugged face matched his broad chest and callous hands.

Unconsciously, I rubbed my breasts on his chest and I heard a sound coming from him. It sounded like a growl. I looked up at him and I saw that his eyes had lost that calm that was like his trademark, in a way. The civilized man had vanished and now I was in the arms of a man who had surrendered completely to his primitive side.

I pulled slightly back, and then my fingers started to unbutton his shirt. I kept staring into his eyes all the time and I could see his pupils getting darker and darker, the light touch of my fingers on his skin arousing him more.

Hardly had I unbuttoned half of the buttons, when Ian, impatient, took my fingers off his shirt, kissed them, and then pulled off his shirt over the head and threw it to the floor with no care about where it would land.

He stared at me, maybe to see my reaction to his chest that simply seemed to have been sculptured with a chisel, or maybe to see if I was as lost as him in what was happening between the two of us.

I noticed he had already taken off his boots only when I saw him with his hand on the zipper of the trousers. He pulled it down with a sudden move. Then he took the trousers and the underwear off at the same time, standing proudly in front of me.

He let me watch him at will for a few moments, then he came towards me with determination, as if the time for games had expired. He pulled me to him forcefully and his mouth found that sweet spot between my shoulder and my neck. A touch there literally made me melt. When he scratched my sensitive skin with his teeth, I got hotter and hotter. I was simply pulsating and I could feel the throbbing in my breasts that had swollen. My nipples were hard and painful and were begging for an attention that was late to come. I felt the pulsations spread lower, as well. They came with the wetness that started to gather in my panties.

The whirlwind of sensations shook me. If he was able to set me ablaze with so little, I was afraid he'd consume me entirely by the end.

Ian let his lips wander lazily on the contour of my cheek and then they continued towards my ear, where he bit my earlobe, which he soothed with the tip of his warm tongue afterwards. He continued his exploration at the back of my ear, and, at the same time, I felt his huge palm covering my breast, stroking it gently at the beginning, then taking the nipple between his fingers and rolling it.

I couldn't stop it anymore and a soft moan left my lips. My eyes closed for a few seconds, but I opened them again when I felt his moist tongue drawing along the seam of the bra, getting underneath, to tease the sensitive skin between my breasts.

Then his mouth slid lower and caught one of the nipples, through the lace of the bra, and started sucking on it to harden it more, and more, until it felt like a pebble, too enlarged to be contained by my skin. It was somewhat painful, but it was a pleasant pain, which made the pulsations and vibrations I felt in the lower part of my body multiply until they became a true sweet torture. By now, my entire body was begging for fulfillment. My blood was running hot.

Ian unhooked my bra and let it fall to the floor and then he literally feasted on one breast and then on the other, alternating with no rules, keeping me always on the edge of the abyss, trying to guess where his mouth would go next. I could only wait and see. Now and then he would lick the hard peak of the breast, some other times he would suckle on it and sometimes I even felt his teeth biting lightly, each time soothing the pain by stroking the spot with his tongue tenderly after his bite.

My body was shivering under his hands and his mouth, and I wish only to feel him entirely, to feel him inside me, to finally be able to go beyond that edge where he kept me suspended.

I fastened my fingers in his hair and I pulled slightly to make him understand what I wanted. He looked up at me, his intense gaze making me shake. Then, he smiled naughtily at me, letting me understand that he hadn't finished with me yet and he still needed to feast on me some more, before going further.

Staring up at me intensely, he blew slightly over the hardened tip of my right breast and when he felt me shivering again, he smiled victoriously. Then, he twirled his tongue around it, pulling it deeper into his mouth and suckled strongly on it. I had to cling to him because, suddenly, I couldn't stand anymore. I was shaking like a leaf and all the nerve endings in my skin had been awoken to a life of tingling and I felt like I was about to shatter in million pieces.

He soothed the erected peak with his tongue once more, and then he moved to the other breast to start the same sweet torture all over again. My fingers were quivering and I hardly could hold onto him anymore. Sparks were going through my entire body and my system was totally short-circuited.

After a while, when my entire world had been reduced to him and to his rough hands and hot mouth on my breasts, his palm slid to my waist, followed by his lips which were leaving wet and hot kisses here and there.

Always here and there, he'd stop to mark my skin with his teeth, each time sending a strong electrical shock through my body.

It got to the point where I almost couldn't exist beyond those sensations. Everything was focused only in those small electrical discharges, and my world was hanging on a thin thread, kept in his big and harsh hands, which were drawing the outline of my body and in those lips which had fascinated me from the first moment I laid eyes on him.

I felt the wet tip of his tongue in my belly button, twirling around, and I jumped out of my skin, making him laugh softly. Then, his palms capped my hips and he drew me towards him a little more. I felt the heat of his lips through the lace of my lingerie. Even through the barrier of cloth I could feel the hotness of his breath and each time he was rubbing his unshaven cheek on me, I would shiver.

I was aware that now he could smell my passion, and I could even hear him inhaling strongly a few times and that made me wetter. I couldn't see but I could imagine what he was doing and that image aroused my desire more, making it stronger, tenser and more intense.

After a while that seemed like a small eternity, his fingers penetrated underneath the edge of my panties and he started pulling them down, maddeningly slowly.

Now, he was already kneeling in front of me to have easier access to the area he was seeking with his mouth. His lips were searching thoroughly each uncovered inch. I felt his teeth scraping longingly the sensitive skin on my hips, followed by his hot tongue that came to appease as always.

Then, I wasn't sure of anything. His mouth was everywhere, leaving wet trails behind, and his fingers were demanding unconditional surrender. His tongue continued to discover all my secrets stubbornly.

My passion was growing every second, with each stroke of his. I felt the need for something more, and Ian didn't disappoint me. The way he made love to me, with his lips and his fingers, was wakening fires in my blood. I felt the tension growing tenfold and becoming unbearable. My skin was burning continuously, as if it were saturated with a myriad of sensations.

I felt my panties sliding lower, following Ian's painfully unhurried movements. Ian was trying to discover even more, to memorize the shape of my legs, of my round behind and the sensitive back of my knees. Nothing was forgotten. Each inch was simply adulated.

I couldn't bear it anymore. The tension was like a tight bundle of nerves, and I was close to exploding. I felt like crying out with joy when Ian finally stood up, took me into his arms and carried me to the bed where he laid me down on top of it carefully.

The moment I felt his body stretching over mine was a true blessing for mine. My body was already prey to the unbearable tightness he had aroused in me. When I felt him sliding inside me, becoming one with me, I purely shattered, having reached my limit long ago.

Ian stopped for a moment, then braced himself on one elbow and his right hand started the torture again, his fingers on the sensitive nub that was throbbing continuously. His mouth took mine masterly and made love to me, his tongue dancing over mine, playing with mine, stroking every corner of my mouth thoroughly.

Then, he descended to my neck, where he started biting me tenderly, suckling each spot his teeth found as an offering. His palm was now stroking my breast and his fingers were playing with my swollen nipple, twisting it, sometimes gently, other times ruthlessly.

I wasn't able to articulate words, but only mere sounds. Ian was laughing blithely, now and then, sometimes he would simply growl, and hearing that guttural sound increased my desire.

When his mouth got to the other breast, I decided it was too much. I felt like I would die because of the tightness coiled inside me and I needed him to start moving inside me, and bring me to fulfillment that very moment. I pushed my hips suggestively and I felt him growing more inside me and that excited me more.

"Please," I managed to whisper, and he raised his head from my breast, looked at me and flexed his hips.

A strong sensation like an electrical charge crossed my body from head to toes. I felt it in my breasts that had swollen painfully, in the belly that was quivering, in the core of my womanhood that was pulsating strongly, and even in my toes that were shaking spasmodically.

Then he began making love to me, alternating the moves of his hips with long kisses on my lips, and then, when his moves became stronger and faster, his lips found my left nipple. Ian started to suckle it in the same rhythm he made love to me. I couldn't resist anymore, I cried out loud, and that bundle of tension that I had had inside me for so long, simply uncoiled and I felt that I was shattered in a myriad of colors.

Ian followed me soon, falling on my body grunting, and his weight felt pleasant on me, adding to my comfort. He gazed at me intensely. He took several seconds to take in my flushed face. Then, he kissed me thoroughly again and only after we lost our breath again, he rolled on his side, taking me with him, holding me tight at his chest as if he couldn't let me go.

We spent a few moments in silence, entwined, trying to catch our breath, while Ian kept stroking my back with a tenderness that I hadn't guessed that he had in him.

I felt content, even happy. It was like I was suspended in a surprising bubble of happiness. I had never felt something so intense, so cathartic.

"It wasn't enough for me," I heard Ian's voice from above me.

I raised my head from his chest and I looked at him. His eyes were half closed, and his forehead was shining with sweat. His five o'clock shadow was making him look dangerous, but his tender touch on my back assured me that I had nothing to fear from him.

"It wasn't enough," he repeated. "I think that even if I make love to you time and time again, it won't ever be enough."

I reached up and I touched his lips with my fingers first, as if I had wanted to memorize their shape, and then I kissed him lightly, but he took my head in his palm and kissed me as if it had been the last time he had the chance to do that. When he let me go, I was dizzy again and my lips were tingling. I put my head back on his chest and in a few seconds, I fell asleep.

CHAPTER 21

When I woke up, it was already evening. It was long past six o'clock. My head was still resting on Ian's chest that was rising rhythmically, sign that he was still deep asleep.

Quietly, so that I wouldn't wake him up, I got out of bed, went to take a shower in the guest bathroom, and then I got dressed in a summer dress and went downstairs to make dinner.

I had marinated some chicken breast and I was just preparing the vegetables, when I heard pounding at the front door. It seemed strange that someone would visit me on a Saturday afternoon, but I went to open the door.

When I opened the door, I found Philippe there. This time he seemed sober. I didn't get to ask him what he wanted because he pushed me forcibly inside, closed the door after him and then knock me down to the floor with a fist.

A few moments he stood over me, watching me with a ruthless resolution, and then he said, "You've destroyed any chance for me, forever. No one will hire me from now on so I have nothing else to do but make sure that you pay, too."

I blinked confused hearing him but I didn't have time to do or say anything because Philippe was already over me, with his hands around my neck and he started to squeeze. I struggled with all my strength and I scratched his face wildly. I kicked him with my feet but I couldn't free myself. Due to the lack of oxygen, I felt that my mind was getting foggier and foggier, and my strength was slackening and, horrified, I realized that it was possible that everything would end like that, stupidly, with Philippe's hands around my neck.

I lost consciousness as the air got thinner and thinner. When I recovered, Ian was holding me, rocking me and, now and then, kissing me.

"Come on, love, you must come back to me," he whispered fervently.

I opened my eyes and for a few seconds we looked to one another and then Ian kissed me lingeringly, hugging me to his heart passionately.

"Philippe?" I asked after I recovered some more and found my voice.

Ian showed me with a sudden flounce of his head where to look and I followed the direction indicated only to see Philippe on the floor with his hands tied.

It looked like Ian had beaten him methodically, because one of his eyes was already swollen and his mouth was bleeding. Nonetheless, he was conscious and now, I could hear him swearing horribly.

"I called the police, so you know. They must come. This time, I really don't care what you say, but the idiot tried to kill you."

"How did you wake up?" I asked.

"I was already up but I was in the shower when he came. Didn't you hear the shower running?"

I shook my head. The rooms were well insulated and therefore, I couldn't hear the shower from the kitchen.

"Well, I heard the commotion only when I came out of the bathroom. Maybe, you'd better go upstairs and bring me something to put on before the police get here," Ian said.

Then I realized that Ian was naked, and his hair was still wet. He let me move carefully, made sure I could stand on my feet and then, he let me go.

Luckily, the police arrived only after I brought his clothes from upstairs and he had the time only to pull his trousers on.

Evidently, lots of questions and explanations ensued, but in the end Philippe was arrested, the police left, and Ian took me in his arms again, keeping me tightly to his chest, and then he said kissing me tenderly, "I thought they wouldn't leave soon enough to have you only to myself."

He held me like that for a long time, kissing me and whispering words I couldn't even understand, and then he asked me, "Why did you leave the bed?"

I looked up at him and answered, "I wanted to make dinner. Luckily, I didn't get to the point to put the chicken into the oven or the dinner would have been burnt by now."

"Yeah, that would have been a serious problem, indeed," he laughed without joy. "I'll make dinner now, and you will rest at the table in the kitchen, sitting nicely down, with a glass of whiskey to keep you company so that you'd recover."

"But I've already recovered, Ian, I can finish cooking."

"No, Meg, you'll have enough chances to cook some other time. Now, it is my turn to take care of you. Are you sure you don't need to go to the hospital?"

"Yes, I'm positive. I'll probably have some horrible bruises on my neck tomorrow, and I'll probably hurt for some time, especially when I talk, it seems, but I think that everything will be all right."

Ian shook his head as if he couldn't believe what had happened, and then he began cooking the chicken I had marinated earlier.

EPILOGUE

Six months later

"Ian, you won't believe it," I cried out with joy and ran into the kitchen where Ian was making breakfast as he would do every morning.

Ian left the spatula on the edge of the pan and came to me. He hugged me tightly and then, he kissed me like he hadn't seen me only half an hour before. He would kiss me like that every morning, but it never got old. Every time, his passion enflamed me.

I was afraid at the beginning that his passion would slowly temper down and then it would vanish and everything would become just routine, but it seemed that my fears were unfounded.

His love for me hadn't diminished in intensity. I could feel that, every day. It actually grew a little more with every day spent together. It was very difficult for both of us to be apart almost all day, but in the evening, when he came back home, we tried to make up for the lost time. We spent most weekends in bed where Ian would always show me something new.

"You're woolgathering again, Meg. I've thought you wanted to tell me something, kitten."

I laughed when I realized that I had completely forgotten why I came in a hurry into the kitchen.

"Oh, yes," I said. "I have just received a letter from that publishing house in New York. They've offered me a contract, look here!" I gave him the envelope and Ian opened it impatiently.

I waited edgily for him to read the letter and then the contract. Ian was very thorough when it came to things like that.

"Fantastic, Meg! It is a very good contract. I knew you'd succeed! You deserve it."

Ian laughed and took me in his arms. He'd always hugged me too tightly but I'd grown used to that and I didn't complain anymore. Then, he started whirling me around making me laugh heartedly.

"We have to celebrate, that's a given," he said after he finally let me stand again. "Here's what we're going to do, Meg. You're going to call these people from this publishing house and tell them that you accept the contract until I finish breakfast…"

"Ian," I interrupted him, "it's still night in New York now. I'll have to wait a few more hours…"

"Oh, yeah, it's just slipped my mind," he said slapping his forehead with his hand. "Of course, you have to call them later. Anyway, we're having breakfast now, and then I'll run to the office to reschedule all my afternoon's meetings. Later on, we'll go out to celebrate. You'll get a cab and come into town, and I'll take care of everything else," he said scooping ng the mushroom omelet out of the pan and putting it onto our plates. Methodic as always, he put the pan into the sink afterwards so that it would soak.

"We can celebrate in the evening, Ian, it's not necessary to ruin your schedule for this…"

"Be serious, love! When it's something important, my schedule doesn't really matter. My clients will survive without me for one day. I am confident about that. Anyway, the time will come when they will have to survive without me for more than one day."

Ian came to me, took my head into his hands, kiss me thoroughly and then, without taking his lips from mine, he whispered, "You are the most important person in my life. No one else counts, Meg. If I have to choose between you and my work, I will always choose you. Even if I'm left with no client in the end, we still can live comfortably, I'm not worried, baby, do you understand?"

I kissed him, too and then I assured him that I understood what his priorities were.

After a breakfast full of laughter and plans, Ian left for the office, and I signed the contract, scanned it and sent it by email, as I had been instructed in the letter, following to send the original by mail afterwards.

I simply had ants in my pants thinking of meeting Ian in the afternoon. Every time we were to meet in town, he made me feel extraordinary. It wasn't only because he was always imaginative and was always doing his best so that we didn't end up stuck in a boring routine. It was also because I knew I held his entire attention no matter what else would happen around, and because we would always communicate. I knew that he constantly put me first.

Around eleven, I heard the bell at the door and when I opened it, I saw a young man holding a huge basket of freesias in one hand and a box of Swiss chocolate in the other. I signed for delivery and then I looked on the card and smiled. Ian had written with his bold hand: *May every day in your life bring you so much joy as today, my kitten! Yours, forever, Ian!*

I burrowed my face in the bunch of freesias and I breathed deeply. I was just crazy about the smell of freesias. I wondered how Ian remembered because I had mentioned that only once, while we were walking in St. Germain's district and I saw freesias planted in front of a house.

I was happy that he wasn't there to see me bursting into tears. I wasn't a very emotional person, but this man always succeeded to stir the most acute emotions inside me.

***

Finally, around noon, I got a text message from Ian informing me that he had ordered a car for me and it would come at one thirty. He also texted that the car was going to drive me to the place where we were supposed to meet.

At one thirty, I left the house and, as clockwork, a car was waiting for me in front of the house. I was driven to Ian's office and when I arrived there, I saw Ian immediately. He was waiting for me on the front stairs of the building. He rushed immediately to open my door, greeted the driver and then led me to his own car.

"I propose we have lunch first, because we must go shopping afterwards," Ian said opening the car door for me and helping me inside. "Of course, I planned a special evening, but, unfortunately, I can't tell you a thing right now, because it is a surprise."

"Really? Nothing?" I asked him after he sat on the driver's seat.

"Nothing, Meg, or otherwise it wouldn't be a surprise, would it?" Ian said smiling, and then, as he used to do almost all the time, he took my fingers and kissed them one by one.

"All right," I said, "then, I'll wait, but you must know that patience is not one of my principal traits."

Ian laughed lightly and kissed me deeply. Then started his car and drove us to the place where we were supposed to have lunch.

We spent almost two hours in an inn on the outskirts of Paris. The inn didn't boast too much luxury, but it sported a special atmosphere and, more importantly, tasty French food.

We discussed about the contract I had just signed, but also about the vacation that Ian thought that we should spend in Greece, on the islands. We went on talking about small things that just made us feel good. We didn't even notice the passing of time.

After lunch, we strolled on the outskirts of the forest for a while. When we got tired, we rested on a log, Ian holding me tightly. We didn't feel the need to talk, just the need to be together.

We came back to Paris only after five o'clock, and Ian stopped the car on Tronchet street, at the lingerie shop Etam. I glanced at him surprised, but he just smiled at me, wearing the same smile he had whenever he felt playful or had a naughty secret he wanted to keep from me for a little longer.

He led me into the shop and asked me to choose a few pieces of lingerie, among which a sexy nighty to surprise him. I measured him strangely. He'd never come with such a request before. However, in the end, I gave in and chose a few sets of lingerie in three different colors and a white silky nighty, which was supported only by two thin straps on the shoulders and stopped at the middle of the thigh, sporting also a slit on the right side.

I didn't even dare to check the prices. I knew the prestige of the shop and I was already a bit worried thinking about my budget. Only the thought that in thirty days I'd get the advance from the publishing house made me calm down. I knew it would cover all my expenses for almost a year so I could afford those few pieces of lingerie.

Apparently, I had fretted for nothing, because Ian insisted to pay for absolutely everything. I didn't feel at ease with his decision, but I knew how stubborn he was and I didn't want an argument in front of the people in the shop. While we were getting out of the shop, Ian kissed the top of my head and said, "You see, this is one of the things I love most about you. You're a very smart girl and you know how to choose your battles."

"You shouldn't think that things will always work in your favor, Ian," I told him, elbowing him in his ribs.

Ian laughed cheerfully and I could read the triumph in his laughter. Then, taking my hand, he led me to his car.

"We still have a stop planned, but it is not necessary that you get out of the car," he said.

We stopped briefly in front of a little shop that displayed scarves, wraps and hats. Ian went inside and came out with a little package in his hand after a few minutes. He hesitated a few moments, then, while I was watching him dumbfounded, he crossed the street and went into a drug store, where he spent almost ten minutes. When he came out, he was carrying a bag in his hand this time.

"I think we have everything we need," he said glancing at his watch. "Right in time. We have to hurry a little to get back to my office."

"Why?"

"Because," he answered teasingly.

"That's not an answer," I replied to him.

"No, it isn't, but that's the only answer I can give you for the time being."

Seeing how stubborn his face looked, I stopped insisting because I knew it was a lost battle. Anyway, I was going to find out soon enough what he had planned.

He drove as fast as possible back to his office and that was never an easy task in Paris. When we got there, he parked his car in his usual spot and started gathering all the bags. Afterwards, he and led me to the front of the building, where, apparently, a driver in a uniform had been already waiting for us for some time. Even though his wait seemed to have been quite long, the driver greeted us respectfully and opened the back door of the car.

I looked at Ian inquiringly but he only winked at me and then bustled me into the car. As soon as both of us had sat down on the back seats, the driver closed the door, and went to his own seat and started the car.

I waited for Ian to say something, but he was content to hold my hand and to whistle lowly, to himself. I abandoned any wish to ask him questions and, instead, I tried to guess where we were going by checking the route.

After just a few minutes, I realized that we were headed towards the Seine, to one of the spots where I had seen yachts anchored before. I looked at Ian inquiringly, but he just smiled at me again, without divulging anything.

We stopped near a small private yacht. The driver opened the car doors, and a man came down off the yacht to welcome us. He greeted us with deference, and then he showed us to the bridge, where a table for two had already been prepared. On the other side of the deck, a quartet was getting ready to perform.

Ian gave the bags to a steward, who took them under the deck, and then, he showed me to the table where he helped me to sit down. Then he took a seat on the other side of the table.

After we sat down, Ian wanted to tell me something but another steward came to the table with a bottle of champagne which he presented to Ian ceremoniously. After Ian approved of the steward's choice, this one started pouring a glass of champagne to each of us and then left us alone.

Apparently, that was the sign that the orchestra waited for, because they started immediately to play one of my favorite songs, Joe Dassin's *Et si tu n'existais pas*.

Ian raised his glass and said, "Let's toast first to your success, which, between you and me, I have never doubted for a single moment. I am sure you'll have more successes in the career you've just begun and I don't want anything more than to be with you along the entire way."

I burst into tears. All my defensive shields had been broken down because of the attention that this man had paid to all the things that mattered to me, no matter how small, and all the efforts he made to offer me a special day.

"Oh, God, kitten, what have I said to upset you?" he panicked.

I shook my head to show him I wasn't upset, but I needed some more time to recover and be able to talk. His eyes showed that he was very worried.

"No, Ian, I'm not upset. The idea is that I am so happy that I couldn't stop my tears. Everything is perfect, even better than perfect."

Ian kissed both of my hands, nibbled at my fingers, and then said,

"What do you say if we toast for you now, and then we dance? Look, the sun is just setting, I'm sure it would be fantastic to dance here, on the deck, surrounded by the sunset …"

I agreed with him and then we toasted. I sipped from the acidulated champagne without taking my eyes off his. I had already known that he had a romantic streak, which was a paradox, actually, as he was a ruthless businessman, from what I had the occasion to see. However, I had never really known the extent of this side of his.

He took my hand and led me to the middle of the deck, when I heard Bryan Adams' song *Everything I do, I'm Doing For You*, another one of my favorite songs. Ian held me tightly against him, and we started swaying slowly in the rhythm of the song.

When the song got almost to the end, Ian whispered, "You know that I also do everything with you in my mind, kitten."

I nodded that I knew and moved closer to him. I needed to feel him more. He held me tighter and then whispered again, "I want you to take my name and wear my ring on your finger. I want us to belong to one another in front of everyone, in front of the law, of the people, of everybody. Will you be my wife?"

Suddenly, my legs refused to move anymore. I stopped and looked up at him in shock. He was serious and was watching me intently.

He let go of me tenderly and then took a box out of his pocket. Opening the box, he kneeled in front of me and held the box out to me.

With tears in my eyes, I couldn't do anything else but reach out to him so that he could put the ring onto my finger.

"I need to hear the words, my love," he whispered.

I nodded that I understood and I said in turn in a voice that shook, "Yes, I will take your name, I will wear your ring and I will be your wife."

He put the ring on my finger with shaking fingers, while everyone on board of the yacht was applauding. I hadn't even noticed that the music stopped and that about seven people were on deck witnessing this moment that surpassed everything I'd ever imagined.

He kissed my hand, stood up, took me in his arms and started to whirl me around like crazy, laughing out loud. Through bursts of laughter and kisses, he was shouting, "Now, you are mine, forever. But for ever and ever."

I was deeply overwhelmed and I had tears running down on my face, which I found very bizarre as at the same time I was laughing as well. When he finally stopped, I was totally dizzy, and he had to carry me in his arms back to the table, where he sat down, keeping me on his lap, decreeing that having dinner like that would be much, much better. Laughing, I approved of his decree. I think that, in those moments, I would have agreed with anything he might have wanted.

Then he told me that we were going to have a cruise overnight and that the entire yacht was available just to us. We were supposed to spend the night in the presidential suite. Then, I finally understood why he had asked me to buy that sexy nighty.

"I think you'd better go first to get ready for the night, and then I'll come too," Ian whispered to me while we were dancing a one last dance.

It was already over eleven at night, and the day had been so full with emotions that, indeed, it was the time to go to bed. Ian kissed me overwhelmingly, and then the steward led me under the deck to our cabin, where the packages that we had brought on board were waiting for me.

The cabin was full of flowers and a diffuse light dressed everything in a romantic nuance, making me feel that this day and night of romance and love would never end. After I finished with my evening rituals, I put on the white nighty I had chosen, and I waited for Ian to come down as well.

He didn't make me wait at all. He seemed to be even impatient, as I heard his heavy steps on the corridor. He came inside, closed the door, and leaning on it, he gazed at me for a few long minutes. He kept looking at me while he took off his coat, and then his shirt, throwing them both in the general direction of an armchair, failing of course to hit his target. He didn't seem to care at all. He just kept looking at me, even when he took off his shoes, socks, trousers and boxers.

Then he came to me, took me into his arms and started to kiss my eyes, then my nose, and only then he took over my lips, while at the same time his hand was sliding over the curve of my breast, and lower, still lower, until he got to the hem of my nighty. He pulled it up, his palm finally reaching my skin and sliding excruciatingly slowly towards the curve of my hip again. At the same time, his mouth descended on my neck where he bit me slightly, then it went lower to the edge of my collarbone. There he scraped my sensitive and tingling skin with his teeth.

Then his lips stopped on the breast he uncovered by pulling the top down. He started to torture the hard peak of the breast, while his abrasive palm kept exploring the curve of my hip, then sliding behind on my back.

He pulled me closer, and he feasted more hungrily from everything I could offer him, and when I thought that I couldn't stand anymore, he took me in his arms, kissed me again lingeringly, and then he told me in a serious voice: "We'll always be like this, kitten. That's something I can promise you."

His eyes were shining intensely in the diffuse light of the cabin and it was like he could read my most intimate thoughts. I believed him with all my heart. After all, he continuously proved to me again and again that he always kept his word.

He headed to the bed where he laid me down carefully, his eyes promising me an unforgettable night. I abandoned myself to his hands, because his hands knew very well to make my body sing with his pure art of lovemaking.

We entwined our bodies as we had already decided to entwine our lives for today and tomorrow and forevermore.

Rowena Dawn writes romance, reads thrillers and watches comedies. She likes walking through the woods but insanely loves the sea. She has a love - hate relationship with her writing and drives her dog crazy whenever she doesn't stop writing to take him out. And yes, she bakes, bread and cakes. Apparently good ones - they're always in demand.

From the Author

I loved writing this book and guessing what Meg would think next. Everyone thinks that Paris is the city of love and I enjoyed setting this love story in this amazing city which offered me so many occasions to build the romance between the heroine and the man she fell in love with.

Also by Rowena Dawn:

Double-Edged (Book One in the Perfect Halves Series)

Becka's Awakening (Book One in The Winstons Series)

Mr. (Almost) Right

Forthcoming:

Matt's Dilemma (Book Two in The Winstons Series)

Eyes in the Dark (Book Two in the Perfect Halves Series)